REAPER

The Indian Territory is a hellhole of lawlessness. Deputies are gunned down in cold blood, and outlaws are trading arms to renegades. In desperation, a bold and secret plan is designed by two senior US marshals — recruit a new and unknown deputy, who can operate independently to hunt down and kill three notorious outlaws in reprisal. But has the right man been selected? Walter Garfield's background seems more than a little shady, and he appears to have his own agenda . . .

Books by Lee Clinton
in the Linford Western Library:

RAKING HELL
NO COWARD
REINS OF SATAN

LEE CLINTON

---◆---

REAPER

Complete and Unabridged

LINFORD
Leicester

First published in Great Britain in 2014 by
Robert Hale Limited
London

First Linford Edition
published 2016
by arrangement with
Robert Hale
an imprint of The Crowood Press
Wiltshire

A catalogue record for this book is available
from the British Library.

ISBN 978–1–4448–3076–7

Published by
F. A. Thorpe (Publishing)
Anstey, Leicestershire

Set by Words & Graphics Ltd.
Anstey, Leicestershire
Printed and bound in Great Britain by
T. J. International Ltd., Padstow, Cornwall

This book is printed on acid-free paper

*For Steve M
Who knows more about the
Western novel than I ever will.*

1

Hellhole of Lawlessness

June–July 1870

The ruthless murder of US Deputy Marshal TJ Sinclair, when on district court business, left his wife destitute and her four children, all under the age of nine, homeless. Deputy Riley Reeves's death ten days later, while escorting three prisoners to Fort Smith for trial, left his young betrothed so stricken with grief that she drowned herself in the creek behind her parents' farm by placing heavy stones in the pockets of her apron.

A week after that Deputy William Foley was ambushed, wounded, taken prisoner then hanged by Mexican bandits who had travelled north to seek sanctuary in the Indian Territory. It was suspected that these were the same

1

outlaws who had robbed a Wells Fargo stage travelling to San Antonio from Austin with a currency transfer from the First Texas Savings Bank.

Foley, who had warrants for the arrest of those involved in the stage hold-up, had been seeking to identify the Mexicans at the time of his brutal murder. His wife had passed away the previous summer from a rattlesnake bite to the hand when reaching for a child's rag doll that had been dropped by their youngest near the water pump. His three daughters were made wards of the State of Arkansas.

All three pitiless murders of these experienced and respected federal officers had occurred in the Indian Territory. They had also happened in the space of less than three weeks. This was to have an immediate and significant impact on the US Marshals Service in a number of ways.

Firstly, a gloom passed over the officers who administered the law from Fort Smith and Fort Worth. They had known all three men well and saw the distress that each passing brought upon their loved ones.

Secondly, a feeling of impotence took hold of the lawmakers in Washington. The federal government was losing the battle to enforce law and order in Indian country, which was now becoming a sanctuary for desperadoes. The influence of these lawless gangs upon the peaceful tribes was also feared, as it might lead to insurrection.

And third, the pool of potential recruits to the US Marshals Service started to ebb like water draining from a leaking rainwater barrel. As US Marshal John Sims was to recall in his memoirs some forty-two years later in 1912:

At that dark time in the history of the US Marshals, the Indian Territory had become a hellhole of lawlessness. So, when Marshal James P. Everette came to me with his radical plan for action, I was willing to entertain any possibility. However, in doing so, there were considerable risks and consequences for all involved.

2

The Proposal

Monday 1 August 1870 — Fort Worth, Texas

Fort Worth District Marshal James Everette leaned forward to confer with Chief Marshal John Sims of Fort Smith.

'The recent killings of three deputies is testimony to the lawlessness of the Indian Territory,' he said quietly, 'and I have received reports that Indian renegades are now being supplied with guns and ammunition by these same outlaws who murdered our officers. The chiefs of the peaceful tribes are losing control of the young warriors and there is talk of uprisings. If we don't do something about this unholy alliance between the outlaw gangs and the Indian renegades we will lose not only more good men but control of the Territory.'

Marshal Sims's face showed his agreement with Everette's assessment. 'Washington believes that law and order has already been lost, but what do you propose we do?'

'I believe I have a solution, but it is contingent on the identification of an independent man amongst our few new recruits.'

'Independent? All our deputies should have that quality. They are expected to work on their own and get the job done.'

'True, but I propose a very different job.' Everette hesitated, then said, 'We have the authority to act and we know who to act against. We even have warrants raised for their arrest, but they are not being served because of the dangers to a lone marshal. The result is that the law is not being enforced and that we are being treated with contempt for our failure.'

Marshal Sims nodded.

'That is why I'm proposing something unusual. Just one truly independent deputy marshal, on his own, with no other tasks. No census duties, or collection of whiskey taxes, or serving of summons for cattle theft. Just this one job.'

'And what job is this?'

'To set an example. One that sends a clear message to those who have killed our marshals. And to those who may consider doing the same in the future.'

'How exactly?'

'My proposal is to identify and select three of the most notorious outlaws for reprisal. The three I have in mind currently exert the most control over the east, west and northern sectors of the Territory; have the greatest influence with the renegades; and have killed a US marshal.'

'Reprisal? Through the courts?'

'No, John,' said Marshal James Everette. 'A marshal could never get one of these men back to Fort Smith for trial. He would be ridden down and killed by those who ride with that outlaw.' Everette lowered his voice a little. 'And anyway, you and I know it would be doubtful if we could get a conviction let alone a hanging. The District Court at Fort Smith is corrupt and it is likely that they would walk free. The courts are not the answer. But reprisal is.'

Marshal John Sims's eyes darted back to Everette. 'Are you advocating that we kill them?'

'I'm advocating that we send the right man into the Territory with a warrant that may be served either dead or alive, and leave it up to that officer to choose which is the most judicious course of action.'

'If he is on his own he will have no choice but to shoot first,' Sims replied, then fell silent in thought before he added, 'Just say we can find such a man and that he, judiciously, removes these outlaws, these three leaders. Then what?'

'We make it known that anyone who

fills their boots will be subject to the same judicious treatment.'

'An unwritten death warrant for those who follow?'

'Precisely.'

'Don't you think that Washington might have a difficulty with this approach?'

James Everette knew he was being gently mocked. 'It depends on how and who is told in Washington.'

Sims looked unsettled.

'John, we must restore law and order.' It was an appeal. 'This way we demonstrate that we are willing to fight fire with fire, and the gangs will become leaderless and disorganized.'

Sims was still showing his unease with the conversation.

Everette spoke slowly to plead his case. 'I have given this considerable thought and believe we owe it to our dead. I have come to the conclusion that there is no other way. I fear that if we don't do this and the situation worsens, then our men will become walking targets for every petty criminal who wants to make a name for himself by killing a US marshal.'

'Do you have someone in mind for this job?'

Everette looked despondent. 'No, at the moment it is just a fanciful idea. But I hold hope that such a man will present himself when I conduct interviews with our last twelve hopeful recruits, tomorrow.'

'Why not use one of our most experienced officers?'

'No, I believe it needs to be someone who is unknown in the Territory. Anonymity will provide protection.'

'Well, *some* protection, I would suggest. At least until he accomplishes his first act of reprisal. However, I suspect that you may have already run out of time and recruits to find such a man.'

'I know, but I still want to seek your agreement, at least in principle, to proceed if I do.'

'And how are you going to broach

this proposal should you find a suitable recruit?'

Everette cast his eyes to the floor. 'I'm not sure.'

Sims shifted in his chair uneasily. 'If I was to agree, how do you propose that we administer this man?'

'I can do it from here at Fort Worth.'

'Not Fort Smith?'

'No, but I would keep you informed.'

Everette's superior thought for a moment. 'If we operate outside the law then we will have no protection from the courts.'

'I know, but what choice do we have? The courts are against us *now*.'

Sims rested back in his chair. 'If you are able to find the right man and he succeeds, then it may be in our interests to demonstrate our achievements to Washington. Our politicians desire success and would be keen to inform our citizens that law and order is being restored and maintained in the most remote and hostile parts of our nation. Their support then becomes our shield, if you understand what I mean.'

Everette smiled a little. 'Yes, but how far should we go in making any of our achievements public?'

'That I don't know, as we could well put this independent deputy at great risk. But at the moment we need to demonstrate to our new masters in the Department of Justice that we are an important executive arm of law and order within our government. If we don't, then we will just become part of the Washington bureaucracy that does little more than hand out census papers, collects taxes, and escorts prisoners. First and foremost we must be seen to enforce the law.'

'On that point, John, we are as one,' said US Marshal James P. Everette. 'So, maybe we need to take bold action.'

Sims sat silently deep in thought then repeated the words *bold action* as he nodded his head.

'Some publicity could also get a message out to the lawless in the Territory that the US marshals were fighting back. And, Lord knows, it would also buck up the sprits of our marshals.'

'Then I have your support?'

'Yes,' said Marshal John Sims softly. 'Yes, you do.'

3

The Last Recruit

Tuesday 2 August 1870 — Fort Worth
'Garfield?' said Marshal James Everette in a tone of questioning that suggested doubt.

'That's right, Walter Douglas Garfield, but call me Walt.' This response showed no concern at any disbelief on display by the inquisitor. If anything it was a mute message of: *I don't much care whether you believe me or not.*

'I just need to get this straight, for the file, as your background seems a little unclear. You say you first came to Texas from California in '63 to join Oswald's Germans, then later Hood's regiment. But your name does not appear in the Appomattox courthouse list of those who surrendered from the three Texas regiments on April 9, 1865. Do you

14

have an explanation for that?'

'Of course I do.'

'And what would that be?' Everette's manner showed that he was shifting from scepticism to suspicion.

Walt leant back, lifting the front legs of the chair off the floor, and smiled.

'I didn't surrender.'

'So where did you go then? South to Mexico with Shelby?'

Garfield's eyes smiled to give his expression a disarming appearance, even a little charming.

'No, I had no mind for such folly. I'd been on one losing side in my life and I had no plans to be on another, so why would I want to run around Mexico with General Joe Shelby and his lost cause?'

'Why indeed? So where have you been for the last five years?'

Walt leant in towards the recruiter and lowered his voice. 'I went prospecting in the Cape River goldfields.'

'Cape River? And where is that, precisely?'

'The colony of Queensland, in the South Seas.'

'The South Seas?'

'The very same.'

'Where the native women wear hula-hula skirts?'

Walt rocked back in his chair. 'No, that was in Samoa.'

'I take it that you didn't strike it rich?'

'No, unfortunately not. My luck deserted me, so I have returned to the nation of my birth.'

'And now you seek employment in your birth nation as a US deputy marshal.'

'Yes I do.'

'How old are you, again?'

'Twenty-six, twenty-seven the end of next month.'

Everette glanced over the upper body of the man who sat before him. Garfield's coat was well worn and open to show a shirt pulling tight at the buttons across a broad chest. Neat stitching at the corner of the right top pocket indicated that it might be his one and only set of clothes.

'You look fit from your gold-prospecting days.'

'As a fiddle.'

'But why?'

'It was hard work.'

'No, I meant, why would you want to join the marshal service? You are a well-travelled and resourceful man. One might even say independent, so why would you possibly want a job upholding the law? There is no fixed salary. You only get paid six cents a mile, whether you're tracking a wanted man or conveying court papers. And you only get two dollars on delivery of a summons or prisoner, and that's regardless of how malicious that man might be. This can be difficult, dangerous and dirty work.'

Walt's face became serious. 'It is time for me to do my bit for the United States of America. You know, protect the community so that they may sleep soundly in their beds.'

'Oh, I see.'

'And I prefer to work from the saddle,' added Walt. 'Just let me loose with a couple of horses and some provisions and I'll get the job done.'

'Do you know what that job is?'

'Upholding the law.'

'How?'

Walt Garfield laughed. 'Chasing after and bringing in wanted men.' Then in a more serious tone, he said, 'I thought a deputy got to keep any state or federal reward money put on a wanted man's head?'

The recruiter closed the file and rested his clasped hands upon the brown cover.

'True,' he said, nodding his head. 'But most of a marshal's work is far more commonplace. Those who do get to chase down a wanted man and fail to deliver him to the courts alive, are left with the privilege of also paying for the funeral costs.'

'What's that work out at?' asked Walt.

'About sixty dollars for a casket,

burial and headstone.'

'Expensive.'

The recruiter let out a long breath. 'I have just one vacant position left to fill, Mr Garfield. Just one. You are the last man to be interviewed and there are eleven potential recruits before you who are all good men of various dispositions, so why should I give this position to you? Can you tell me that?'

Walt thought for a minute. 'I could say because I am the best man, but I don't know if that would satisfy you.'

The recruiter nodded in agreement.

'So, why not approach it this way.' Walt looked down at the brass nameplate on the desk that read J.P. Everette. 'John,' he said.

'James,' corrected Everette.

Walt seemed to dismiss the correction as being of no consequence. 'Why don't you just cull out those who are not suitable for this type of work? Then we can see who we have left.'

'Cull?'

'Yes, just remove those names that

aren't suitable and see who is the last man standing.'

'And that will be you?'

Walt grinned. 'I'll bet on it.'

Everette leant back a little and folded his arms. 'Go ahead then.'

'How many men on your list are married?'

'Half,' replied the recruiter quickly without making any reference to the files on his desk.

'Erase them. Apprehending armed offenders who prize their freedom above all else is not a job for a married man.'

'Why not?'

'It involves the taking of risks and married men are reluctant to take chances if it leaves their family without a breadwinner.'

The recruiter's face remained expressionless. 'So we are down to six.'

'How many from that six are over thirty-five?'

Everette thought, but only for a moment. 'Four.'

'Scratch them off your list, too. This is a young man's game. Long hours in the saddle, living rough and on meagre rations. It'll kill 'em.'

'Some of our best and most experienced marshals are over thirty-five.'

'I'm sure that is so, but they are the smart ones who have had the opportunity to cut their teeth in their youth, and who now know how to use that hard-gotten expertise.'

'So, that leaves just two. You and one other. Do I toss a coin?'

Walt held up his hand as if to take an oath.

'No, I wouldn't do that. The odds are even that you'll get it wrong. I've learnt never to put my trust in fate.'

Everette's face pinched just a little to suppress a smile.

'Is the other man an idealist?' asked Walt.

'All of them have stated that they understand the importance of being a fine citizen and setting a good example in upholding the law. So, aren't you also an idealist, Mr Garfield?'

'I used to be, but I learnt that it is better to be more practical.'

'And when did you convert to this more practical approach to life?'

'In '65 when I found myself on a losing side.'

'So how does this practical approach work?'

Walt lowered his voice a little and leant in, his arm resting on the edge of the desk.

'An idealist will want to arrest his man face to face and read him the charges that are being laid against him. He will want to demonstrate the rightfulness of the law and the power of his position to enforce it. While, on the other hand, a practical man will take a more shrewd approach. He knows that there is a time when every man will drop his guard, be it when he is asleep, drunk or just plain dozy. Pulling a man from his bed when he is in a stupor, or out of a hot tub when he is engaged in some hokey-pokey with a gal, may not seem heroic but you still get your man, and you do it with a minimum of fuss.'

Marshal James Everette tapped the file cover with his finger to make the only sound in the small room and tried to suppress a smirk.

'You have a persuasive tongue, Mr Garfield.'

Walt smiled. 'I thank you for the compliment.'

'How would you like to work on your own?'

'I thought all marshals worked on their own.'

'Not at first. We pair newcomers with an older hand. It helps to keep them alive.'

'Oh, I won't need any of that nursemaiding.'

'You didn't let me finish. How would you like to work on your own in the Indian Territory?'

Walt didn't hesitate. 'That would suit me dandy.'

'Don't be in such a hurry; you should hear me out first.'

Walt drew his chair in a little and said, 'Fire away.'

'Your employment will keep you independent of any of the other marshals also working in the Territory. You will report directly back to me, and just to me. This is not normal: it is a very special case.'

'Very special and independent,' repeated Walt with a smile.

'You seemed pleased with that?'

'Couldn't be more pleased if I'd arranged it myself.'

'If I were you I'd put a hold on any celebrations until you hear my proposal, as you may wish to refuse what I have on offer.'

'An offer?'

'Yes, an offer.'

'The US Marshals Service sure is different from the army. When I was in uniform you just jumped when they said jump.'

'Don't worry; we also say jump but in this case it is — '

Walt cut in: 'Very special.'

'Yes,' said Everette a little uneasily. He then took a deep breath. 'The Indian Territory is now the most lawless place in our nation and I . . . ' he stopped to correct himself, 'we, fear that it might not only get worse but become irredeemable. Outlaw gangs are now well established and known to work with each other.'

'Like a cartel?' suggested Walt.

'Yes, cartel,' said Everette, impressed with the use of the term by Walt. 'This relationship has extended to Indian renegades, who are being supplied with arms and ammunition.'

Walt tapped a finger to his lips as if to keep his silence.

'Three gang leaders have been identified, who present the most concern to law and order in the Territory. For our purposes let's call them A, B and C. Each one is a violent man who has repeatedly broken the law by theft of property or cash. Each has used intimidation against honest settlers in the Territory to move them on or have them pay for protection. Each has sold arms and ammunition to renegade Indians. And each has had a direct involvement in the murder of a US marshal.'

'Busy men,' mumbled Walt under his breath.

'Yes, very busy. But I have a plan to stop them and it involves you, should you wish to accept this last vacancy I have on offer to become a US deputy marshal.'

'Precisely what do you want me to do, with Mr A, B and C?'

Everette drew in a short breath through his teeth, then abruptly said, 'Kill them.'

Walt's head jolted back in an instant. He then reached up and pulled on his ear, pressing his lips together as if he was trying to hold something back. Then he asked, 'Is that legal?'

'Let's just say that it is borderline.'

'How borderline?'

'Well, provided you and I don't get caught, we should be fine.'

'Oh, *that* borderline,' mocked Walt. 'And all for no fixed salary and six cents a travelled mile?'

'No, this is an altogether different arrangement.' Everette was serious. 'Your personal remuneration will be fixed at thirty dollars per month and the normal payment of six cents per mile.' He kept his eyes on Walt. 'And you get to retain the reward, if successful.'

'And what is that reward, exactly?' asked Walt.

'One thousand dollars per head.'

'And you throw in the horses and provisions to go and find these three?'

'Yes, and some additional funds for expenses.'

'Then I'm in.'

'Are you sure?' asked Everette firmly.

Walt smiled. 'I'm sure all right.'

Everette slowly extended his hand to Walt.

'Then, Deputy Garfield, welcome to the US Marshals Service.'

4

In a Heartbeat

Wednesday 3 August 1870 — Fort Worth

Everette took a small brass key from his vest pocket, opened the left-hand drawer of his desk and withdrew three sets of papers. He dropped them, one at a time, on to the surface of the bureau with a smack. Around each bundle was a black ribbon tagged with a large single letter. The first was marked A, the second B and the last C.

'These are the warrants and the authority for arrest, dead or alive. A for Frank Allen; B for Louis Bolan, a Frenchman from Louisiana; and C for a Mexican named Eloy Cobos.'

'A Frenchman, Bo-lan,' Walt emphasized the name with an accent, 'and a Mexican? What are they doing in the

Indian Territory?'

'The same as the other outlaw gangs. Hiding from the law and taking every opportunity to rob and steal from anyone they can find. The Territory can be lucrative; cattle move through it to the markets in Kansas, and soon the railroads will extend their tracks to the south. Their surveyors are already mapping a corridor so that rail may be laid to transport people south and cattle north. This is land with rich potential for our nation.'

Walt remained silent.

Everette continued: 'If, after serving these papers, it was to occur that the accused could not be arrested peaceable, then you would be at liberty by virtue of these papers to use your best judgement, judiciously.'

'Forgive me,' said Walt slowly. 'I'm a little new to the law. You said, use my judgement judiciously. What does that mean, exactly?'

'That you may serve these papers to a dead man.'

'And these papers allow me to do that?'

'In a legal sense. All you have to do is just serve them.'

'Legal sense?'

'One that is yet to be tested.'

'OK,' said Walt slowly. 'So, in a legal sense, it doesn't matter if the man I am serving them to is already dead?'

Everette nodded. 'Legally, but you need to report to me directly, as soon as it is practicable to do so after you have been successful. It will allow me to protect you as I have authorized the raising of these warrants.'

'Report how exactly?'

'By telegram. A number of settlements in the Territory are now on the wire, and where that is not available most other settlements have a courier service to the nearest telegraph station.'

'So I write you a note and hand it to some mail service clerk saying I have just killed a man?'

'No, you write out a telegram that just uses the letter A, B or C, saying that papers have been delivered successfully. Successfully, meaning — '

'I got it,' interrupted Walt. 'You've given this considerable thought, haven't you?'

'I have.'

Walt grinned a little. 'So how do we get this circus on the road?'

'You will be provided with four horses and enough provisions for six weeks. We can also help you out with some clothing.'

'And where do I go with my four horses, provisions and new outfit? The Indian Territory is kind of big.'

'Seventy thousand square miles,' said Everette.

'That's big,' said Walt.

'You should start your search in Atoka on the eastern side of the Territory, and then be prepared to head north or west. Do you know the country at all?'

'I been through it with my parents when we went to California, but I was just a tot then.' Walt seemed to get lost for a moment as he reflected on that time, and then said, 'Is that all you've got, a starting point?'

'It is an important centre and will allow you to ask around. If you find one, then it will most likely lead to the others, as all three have done business together at some time. But you will need to be careful when making enquiries.

'I have authorized an imprest account of one hundred and fifty dollars in cash, of which every dollar is to be accounted for, so keep an accurate record of expenditure.

'I have also authorized that you draw twelve turban-head gold pieces. They are highly prized and can be used at your discretion. They will buy you information.'

Walt smiled. 'Seems like I'll be a cross between an accountant and a banker.'

'You will be a US deputy marshal with a badge, and that alone can get you killed. If you are also known to be carrying cash and gold coins then you will invite harm. You are embarking on dangerous business.'

Walt nodded and tried to look thoughtful.

Everette lowered his voice a little. 'I myself report to just one man, the chief marshal at Fort Smith, who will be keen to demonstrate to Washington any success.'

Walt half-nodded in agreement. 'Keep the big bosses happy, eh?'

Everette paused for a second or two, then said, 'Washington will also be keen to demonstrate their success to the American people.'

'Their success?' said Walt. 'Will it be their success?'

'That's how these things work,' said Everette.

'And what does that mean, in a word or two?'

'It means that your success, our success, will be reported as their success in the newspapers.'

'A lot of successes,' mumbled Walt.

Then he said, 'Telling a lot of people could make my job a little tricky, don't you think? Riding around the countryside, cashed up and knocking over certain prominent villains so that one and all can read about it in the papers back east, seems kinda public.'

'Yes,' said Everette, 'but there is no other choice. We need to set an example.'

'An example?' questioned Walt.

Marshal James P. Everette nodded. 'We need to demonstrate that when the law is broken, especially against those whose duty it is to uphold our statutes, then there will be consequences. And we need to do it with urgency.'

'With urgency,' repeated Walt.

'Yes. Now that I have found the man I have been searching for, we must act with speed,' said the marshal.

'Searching for me?' said Walt slowly. 'Why me?'

'You are an independent and well-travelled man, and your past is a mystery. Therefore you are unknown to those you are about to hunt down and their protectors.'

'And if they did know me?' asked Walt.

'Then they would kill you in a heartbeat.'

5

Silence

Thursday 4 to Saturday 6 August
Walt used the whole of the next day preparing for the journey. Provisions were drawn from the Fort Worth quartermaster and packed into taupe canvas sacks. Two of the four horses allocated to him were then fitted with carry harnesses to sling-load these sacks.

The funds, in cash and gold coins, were signed for by Walt directly from Marshal Everette, who also gave him a field notebook to account for expenditure. In it he was required to record all miles travelled, along with any important occurrence.

Walt flicked open the cover, looked at the lined pages and wondered if there would be any time left for the job he'd been given, after he'd completed the required daily paperwork.

The final item issued to him came from the armoury. Walt's personal belt pistol was a Navy Colt cap-and-ball .44, while his rifle was a Henry Model 1866 that took .44 rim-fired metallic cartridges. Both weapons were showing signs of wear, but they were serviceable and well maintained. However, when the armourer inspected the weapons for suitability, he offered the newly appointed US deputy a Model 3 Smith & Wesson revolver to replace his Navy Colt.

'It takes .44 metallic cartridges,' advised the armourer, 'but not rim-fired; this is centre-fired pistol ammunition.'

Walt picked up the handgun and became mesmerized by its slick look and feel.

'I've heard stories about these,' he declared as his eyes caressed the blue-black metal frame of the pistol. Then he added with a grin, 'Don't this make life a hell of a lot easier. Where did it come from?'

'Left over from an army field trial some six months ago. Word is that they want a bigger cartridge.'

'What are they shooting?' asked Walt. 'Buffaloes?'

'Indians,' was the deadpan reply from the armourer.

'It will do me,' said Walt. 'If the first round won't work, then I'm sure the second will.'

But, much as Walt had taken to his new Smith & Wesson, he decided to retain his old Colt and take it with him, if only out of sentimentality.

The following morning, without ceremony, he left for Gainesville just before first light and didn't look back. He rode north with the urgency that Everette had impressed upon him and completed the sixty-mile journey just before last light by changing horses every two hours.

He resumed his journey to Atoka the next morning, getting under way well before first light this time, so that he could complete the seventy-six miles by the end of the day.

When Walt dismounted at McBride's livery and stock stables on Court Street it was dark and he was a little saddle-sore. The town was quiet and the only signs of life came from the oil lamps in the front-room windows facing along the main street. He paid for his four horses to be placed under cover, along with an extra stall to store his supplies. As he pulled the saddle blanket from his mount and shook out the dust, McBride the owner carried over a second oil lamp to assist him with his duties.

'See you've been riding hard,' said McBride as he placed the lamp on a hook above the stall. 'You surveying for the railroads or just passing through?'

It was a nosy question and Walt knew he was fishing.

'Something like that,' he said as he folded the blanket and laid it on the side rail.

'Will you be staying long?' asked McBride.

'Not sure, but at least a day, maybe two to rest the horses — and me.'

'Come far?'

Walt looked around. 'You got a brush?'

The stable owner turned round, then reached over, took a brush from on top of the railing post and handed it to Walt.

'Obliged,' said Walt. He began brushing down the hindquarter, his face turned away.

'So what brings you to Atoka?'

Walt kept brushing in silence, before he eventually said, 'I'm looking for a man.'

This time the stable owner let the silence hang before he asked, 'Which man would that be?'

'A man by the name of . . . ' Walt paused but kept brushing, then said, 'Taylor. Jason Taylor.' He brushed some more. 'Has he passed through your stables?'

'Not that I can recall,' said the owner. 'But my memory can be faulty at times.'

Walt smiled, but it was unseen by the owner.

'Mind you, a man can change his name when he is travelling. What does this man Taylor look like?'

'Older,' said Walt. 'Some grey in his hair, but still hard and fit. Around my height, a little heavier and travelling with a woman. A Mexican woman.'

The only sound in the stall was the strokes of the brush.

Walt continued: 'I would have thought that they'd be easy to spot.'

More silence.

'I could make it worth while if your memory needs a nudge,' he added.

'How?' asked McBride.

'I can sell you one of these horses, cheap. I only need three.'

'Another horse I don't need and that one over there has a federal brand on it.' The owner nodded towards the first horse that Walt had stripped.

Walt kept his head turned away to hide his surprise and annoyance at being tripped up over such a simple thing as the mark on one of his horses. He sucked in a quick breath.

'Was once,' he said. 'Not any more. Got it at auction in Fort Worth.'

'They should have rebranded it before sale.'

'Must have forgot.' Then Walt said, 'I've got a little cash on me.'

'Oh, yeah?' said the owner.

'It might help your recollection.'

'Could, but depends on how much is on offer.'

Walt knew he was being squeezed. 'I have a gold turban-head if you were to tell me what I need to know.'

'You must want this Taylor fella real bad to go offering a gold piece for his whereabouts. What do you want him for?'

'Some unfinished business.' Walt pulled up the hind leg of his horse as if to inspect the two-day-old shoe.

'Business that must be worth a lot

more than a gold piece.'

'Uh-huh,' said Walt as he lowered the hoof. 'But the piece is also to buy your silence. I don't want Taylor knowing that I have been asking after him.'

'You want to surprise him, then?' said the owner.

'Oh yes, I want to do that all right,' said Walt.

'Anyway, I haven't seen any man travelling with a Mexican woman, so I guess that's that — worse for me.'

Walt straightened up and looked across at the owner.

'At least you're an honest man, or you could have taken my money and sent me off on a wild-goose chase, so for that I'm obliged.' Walt watched closely and saw that McBride accepted the compliment with pride.

'But,' he continued as he placed the horse brush back on the railing post, 'if you might know someone who could point me in the right direction, it could still be worth that gold piece.'

The livery owner thought for a moment.

'Ernie Brockman follows the comings and goings of immigrants. Then there's McSweeney the storekeeper, he supplies the army and hears what they have to say.' He scuffed his foot kicking back some straw. 'Or you could ask Frank Allen. He travels around a lot. He's a man of prominence in these parts.'

Walt had to stop the surprise from showing on his face when he heard the name Frank Allen, so he silently held his breath before saying: 'A travelling man? He should know something. Where,' he sucked in another quick breath, 'could I find Mr Allen?'

'He doesn't get around much now; he's not been too well. He came here to see the doc, but he spends most of his time in the saloon.'

'Which saloon?'

'We only have one.'

Walt extracted a turban-head gold coin from the top pocket of his shirt where he had placed it for this very eventuality, then handed it to the owner, who showed genuine surprise.

'I don't believe I deserve this,' said McBride.

Walt shook his hand with a firm grip. 'Remember, it is not just payment for information, but for your silence as well,' said Walt.

The owner looked down at the coin and smiled.

'Silence,' repeated McBride. 'Well, you certainly have that.'

6

At Rest

A Little Later

When Walt walked into the Hotel Atoka
with his saddle valise over his arm and
clutching his rifle along with a small
calico bag of toiletries, the place
seemed completely deserted. Then he
noticed a lone figure dressed in a dark
suit at the other end of the bar hunched
over his drink.

Walt glanced around, looking for any
other signs of life, but there was none.
The only suggestion that anyone else
might be around was a feather duster
and cleaning cloth, which lay upon the
surface of the bar immediately before
him.

Walt was to idly reflect on this
situation later and wonder if he should
have taken his chances there and then.

After all, McBride at the livery stable had told him that he would find Frank Allen in the saloon and this was the only saloon in town. All he needed to do was draw his pistol and conceal it beneath the valise, establish the man's identity as Frank Allen, and shoot him dead. In hindsight it would seem such an uncomplicated and convenient solution. However, that such good fortune would deliver to Walt his first victim alone and just a handful of steps away was beyond all belief, so he hesitated.

This indecision that evening in the saloon was to be followed by some lamentation. Had he shot the man at the end of the bar, with no eyewitnesses present, it would have saved him considerable time and effort, not to mention expense. But the opportunity was lost when he leant over the feather duster and the crumpled cleaning cloth and rang the small brass bell on the counter to summon attention.

The man at the end of the bar didn't

look up; he just said in a slurred mumble, 'Ring again, he's out the back,' then poured himself another drink.

Walt rang a second time and waited before a portly man arrived through the side door to offer his apologies for his absence.

Walt asked for a room, then added, 'Just the one night.'

'You want me to show you to your room now?'

'I'll have a drink first,' replied Walt.

'Whiskey?'

'Do you have any rum?'

'Some.'

'Cuban?'

'Not out here. Only Medford.'

'You'd have to go to Orleans for Cuban,' said the lone figure at the end of the bar, his voice gravelled and slow.

'So what are you drinking, friend?' asked Walt.

The lone drinker didn't give a reply.

The hotelkeeper said quietly, 'He's

drinking brandy. Do you want a brandy?'

'No,' said Walt. 'A whiskey will do.'

'I've got Peppers from Kentucky.'

'Fine,' said Walt. He placed his valise, rifle and calico bag down upon the floor.

'Peppers is good,' came the voice from the end of the bar. 'Better than brandy wine.'

Walt tried again. 'Then let me buy you a Peppers.'

'No,' came the reply with a cough. 'The physician says that brandy is much better for a man in my condition.'

'What condition is that?' asked Walt.

He didn't get an answer, but as the hotelkeeper poured Walt his drink, he whispered, 'Consumption.'

Walt started to fumble through his coat pocket to pay.

'As a house guest I can put it on your bill, if you like?'

It was an old trick and Walt had been stung with it before. What was put on the bill and what was drunk was often impossible to recollect. But he concluded that he needed to stay on the right side of the proprietor, especially if he was going to kill one of his patrons.

'OK,' he said. He put the whiskey to his lips and smelt the mix of burnt oak, earth and caramel, then swallowed. 'Smooth.'

'It's my best,' said the hotelkeeper with some pride. 'You want another?'

Walt nodded as the warmth of the alcohol took hold.

'Expensive too,' came the voice from the end of the bar.

'The good stuff always is,' said Walt, his mind searching for a plan. He picked up the second glass. Just before he put it to his lips he said, 'You wouldn't be Mr Frank Allen, would you?'

The lone figure stiffened and dropped his right hand out of sight. Walt knew that it had gone down to his gun.

The hotelkeeper stepped back from the bar.

'Mr McBride at the livery said that you might be able to help me. I'm looking for someone travelling through the Territory. His name is Jason Taylor.'

The figure at the end of the bar relaxed, just a little. Hesitantly the hotelier returned to the bar.

'He's with a Mexican woman,' added Walt.

'No,' came the response with a cough. 'I've not seen or heard of those two. Have you, Bert?'

The hotelkeeper shook his head. 'No, not here.'

'Then I'm out of luck,' said Walt and finished his second drink.

'Another?' asked the hotelkeeper.

'Why not?' said Walt. He turned towards the end of the bar and said, 'My name's Walt Garfield.'

He received no response.

'You are Frank Allen, aren't you?'

'I am.'

'McBride also thought that I should ask the storekeeper or a man named Brockman, as they might know.'

'If Bert hasn't heard of your man and his woman, then McSweeney won't have either. As for Brockman, he's a churchman. Is this man you're looking for a churchgoer?'

'No,' said Walt.

'Then you've drawn a blank,' coughed Frank Allen as he poured another brandy.

Walt waited until the coughing stopped, then watched as Frank leant over to one side to spit into the brass spittoon down by his feet. As he did so, Walt could see the blood mixed in the saliva.

'Not good,' whispered the hotel-keeper.

'No,' agreed Walt.

'You should go to Henrietta, not Atoka to find out who's running around the Territory. In Henrietta they seem to know what's going on everywhere, and they talk about it, a lot.'

'Never been to Henrietta,' said Walt.

'Nor have most people, but now the Kiowa have been put down the Anglos are returning.'

'Henrietta,' Walt repeated. 'I'll keep that in mind.'

Frank went to speak, but stopped, lowering his head as if desperate to catch his breath. He then put his hand up as if to stop Walt and the hotelkeeper from talking to him. He shook slightly, let out a series of small half-coughs, then suddenly collapsed on to the floor with a thump.

'Good God!' said the hotelkeeper.

Walt stepped quickly across to the prostrate figure and lifted Frank's head from the floor. Around each corner of his mouth was red bubbling froth, and blood could also be seen on the whiskers of his moustache.

'Throw me that cloth,' said Walt.

The hotelkeeper seemed startled.

'The cloth on the bar.'

After some hesitation the hotelkeeper grabbed at the bar cloth and threw it towards Walt.

Walt caught the rag and wiped Frank's mouth, leaving a red stain on the fabric.

'You got any smelling-salts?' called Walt, just as Frank revived and started to speak.

'Drink,' he mumbled.

'Water,' called Walt. 'Get some water.'

'No,' coughed Frank. 'Brandy.'

'Are you sure?' asked Walt.

'Brandy,' repeated Frank. 'I've paid for that bottle and by God I'm going to drink it.'

'OK,' said Walt. 'Pour Mr Allen another brandy from his bottle.'

The hotelkeeper poured the drink, walked round from the other side of the bar and passed it to Walt with a shaking hand.

'I thought he'd dropped dead,' he said.

'Not yet,' said Frank just before Walt got the glass to his lips.

'Where's the doctor's?' asked Walt.

'Six doors up on this side,' said the hotelkeeper, 'next to the general store.'

'Go get him,' said Walt.

'No,' said Frank. 'He charges a dollar to call. Help me up, I can walk, but I need another drink first to muster my strength.'

Walt looked down in amazement at the glass that was now empty.

'No,' he said. 'Best we get you to the doc right away.'

Walt pulled Frank to his feet and was surprised how light he was for his height. When he got him to the doctor's, where he was propped up in a large chair with two pillows behind his head, and his shirt was opened by the physician so he could tap upon his chest, Walt could see why. Frank Allen was all skin and bones.

'He's been drinking,' said the doctor.

'Brandy,' said Walt. 'He said you recommended it.' Then he added, 'For a man in his condition.'

'A nip before bedtime,' said the doc. 'Not a bottle at a time. He has tuberculosis and is dying. Drinking like a fish will just hasten his end.' The doc looked around the small room. 'Hand me my bag.'

Walt handed him a small black

leather satchel, which was on the table beside him. The doctor removed a small bottle and handed it to Walt.

'Give him this.'

Walt read the side of bottle, which said, *Soothing Syrup. Cures coughs, colic and cramps*.

'Where are you going?' he asked.

'I may have to deliver a child, just at the end of the street. I'll return as soon as I can. After the medicine just leave Frank to rest and don't let him have any more brandy. It will kill him.'

Walt went to protest, but it was too late, the doctor was gone.

Walt looked at Frank, who seemed to have fallen into a deep sleep with his head hanging forward. So, quietly and slowly, he placed the small bottle of syrup on to the table, then leant in and listened to Frank's breathing. It was very faint as Walt carefully but firmly grasped the top pillow with both hands and started to ease it out from behind Frank's head.

'Drink,' came the call from Frank, startling Walt.

'Are you comfortable?' said Walt quickly as he pushed and prodded the pillow back into place.

'Drink,' repeated Frank.

'I have it,' said Walt. He grasped and held up the small bottle of syrup.

Frank lifted his head slightly to focus.

'Not that shit. Brandy.'

'Brandy?' repeated Walt.

'Damn it,' said Frank between coughs, 'I paid for that bottle.'

'Hold on, Frank,' said Walt. 'I'll be right back.'

When he re-entered the hotel four guests now stood at the bar, drinking. Walt looked around for the items he had placed on the floor but they were gone. He then caught the eye of the hotelkeeper, who hurried over to him.

'Where's my kit?' asked Walt in a whisper.

'It's safe, out the back,' whispered the hotelkeeper. 'How is Frank?'

'He wants his bottle of brandy.'

'Are you sure? He didn't look in any fit state to drink.'

Walt looked around quickly. 'Just get it, and give me a glass.'

'You can't carry a bottle down the street in public,' said the hotelkeeper. 'We have ordinances against that, and that's the mayor over there. It could mean my licence.'

'It's dark outside,' said Walt.

'It doesn't matter,' said the hotelkeeper.

'For God's sake, man, get me my wash bag; I'll put it in there. And my saddle valise, get that too, I need some papers from it.'

The hotelkeeper returned with the valise and calico sack, which still held Walt's razor, shaving brush and soap.

'You could have emptied it.'

The hotelkeeper seemed about to respond.

'It doesn't matter, give it here.' Walt stuffed the brandy bottle into the bag and opened the valise. He pulled out the papers with the letter 'A' marked just below the ribbon, and placed the sheaf inside his jacket. Then he picked up the glass and left.

'You'll need to bring the glass back,' called the hotelkeeper.

Walt was about to say *put it on my bill*, but stopped short. Back at the doctor's quarters, he was just inside the door when the doctor followed him in.

'False alarm,' said the physician, then looked down and saw the glass in Walt's hand. 'What's that for?'

'I . . . I went back to the hotel for it,' stuttered Walt, 'for the syrup.'

'I have glasses here, you should have looked.'

Walt said nothing as the doctor moved over to where Frank sat crumpled in the chair. The doctor picked up Frank's right hand and felt around the wrist while making small grunting gestures. He did the same to the left wrist.

'Frank Allen is now at rest,' he said at last. 'He is dead.'

7

The Doctor

A Minute Later

'Dead? *Dead* dead?' said Walt.

'That's the only dead I know,' said the doctor.

'But he was alive before.'

'Just. But now he's dead.'

Walt stepped back so that he could sit down upon a small wooden bench against the wall. He stared at Frank slumped in the chair.

'It's been a long day,' he said. 'I rode up from Gainesville.'

'Good ride to do in a day,' said the doc.

'I've come here to serve papers on Frank.'

'What sort of papers?'

'A warrant for his arrest. I'm a US deputy marshal.'

'You're too late,' said the doctor. 'You can't serve papers on a dead man.'

Walt looked down at his boots as his thoughts swirled.

'It was worth a small fortune to me. He had a reward on his head.'

The doctor glanced over at Walt with interest, squinted a little, then asked, 'How much?'

'Five hundred,' replied Walt.

The doctor whistled quietly. 'Five hundred dollars. I would have to deliver a lot of offspring to make that, at six dollars a brat.'

'Over eighty,' said Walt without looking up.

The doctor thought for a moment, then said, 'You're right, over eighty.' He whistled again before asking, 'So what happens to the reward, now?'

Walt kept looking at the floor. 'Oh, if it goes unclaimed then it is given back to the government in Washington.' Then he added, 'To spend on politicians' entertainment, I guess.'

'They'll do that with the money?

Entertain themselves?' asked the doctor.

'And more, I fear,' said Walt. 'There are houses in Washington where officials can go for discreet recreation after they dine.'

'I've heard that,' said the doc through tight lips. 'But is it paid for from the public purse?'

Walt scuffed a boot. 'Afraid so.'

'That doesn't seem right,' said the doctor, 'all those officials — '

Walt cut in. 'Having all that recreation?'

'Yes, it's just not right,' said the doctor in disgust.

'If only there was some way,' said Walt. 'Some way still to serve the papers, then we could both benefit and have a little recreation ourselves.'

'We?' said the doctor. 'You would be willing to share some of that reward?'

'Sure,' said Walt. 'Fifty-fifty would be fair, if only it were possible.'

'Exactly what would you need to do?'

'If Frank was still alive, you mean?'

'Yes.'

'I would firstly have to identify him as Frank Allen.'

'I can vouch for that,' said the doctor with open enthusiasm.

'Then I would have to present him with the papers for his arrest.'

'Then what?' asked the doctor.

'Then, I'd take him into custody and escort him back to either Fort Smith or Fort Worth.'

'Fort Worth is a better ride,' said the doctor.

'Yes, it is, for a living prisoner,' said Walt. 'But not now.'

The doctor shook his head. 'What a lost opportunity.'

'Mind you,' said Walt, 'had Frank refused to accept the papers, or sought to abscond rather than be taken into custody, and had I then been forced to shoot him dead, then the five hundred dollars would still be paid.'

'Really?' said the doctor with renewed interest.

'Oh yes, under such circumstances all

the requirements of the warrant would have been met.'

'You know,' said the doctor, 'I could register the death . . . ' He stepped in closer to Walt, slowly sat down on the small bench beside him and whispered, 'as a shooting.'

Walt looked away and pressed his lips tight to suppress any hint of a smirk.

'Well,' he said, 'that wouldn't hurt Frank none, would it? I mean, he's dead, isn't he?'

'That's right,' agreed the doctor. 'No harm in it for Frank.'

'But what if someone examined the body and found that he didn't die of a wound?' asked Walt.

The doctor thought for a minute, then said, 'Yes, we could be found out if that were the case.'

As the doctor went to stand Walt clutched at his arm.

'I could shoot him.'

The doctor turned sharply with surprise.

'I just have to put one shot in him,'

explained Walt. 'Frank won't know. He's dead.'

The doctor was looking decidedly uneasy.

'No, that doesn't seem right, shooting a dead man.'

'No,' said Walt, 'I expect you're right. Mind you, we'd never make an easier two hundred and fifty dollars each again in our lifetimes. I have the authority to serve the warrant and you have the authority to sign the certificate of death. Both are needed to claim the reward. It would be a partnership.'

'Two hundred and fifty dollars.' It was said slowly, as though in a dream before the doctor seemed to come back to his senses. 'Still, it just doesn't seem right.'

'So close. It was only a matter of minutes,' said Walt. He stood up, went over to the body and touched the hand. 'He's still warm.'

'We can't turn back the clock though, can we?' said the doctor.

'No, but we still have time,' said Walt.

'If we were to act now.'

'How?'

'I could deliver the papers, which you could witness, Frank could refuse and I could fire a shot. All done and dusted in a jiff. Except for the paperwork, but that has to be done anyway.'

The doctor thought for a little before he said, 'Have you ever done anything like this before?'

Walt shook his head. 'No, but there is a first time for everything, and this one seems simple enough, for two hundred and fifty dollars.'

'Two hundred and fifty dollars,' repeated the doctor. 'I could do with that. It would allow me to travel back east.'

'Where to?'

'New York.'

'Ahh, New York. I like New York. Lots of recreation in New York. So, you want I should do it?'

'I don't know. It's tempting, but — '

'OK then,' said Walt. 'Let me act it out and if you say stop at any time, then that's what I'll do. OK?'

The doc slowly half-nodded in agreement.

'Ready?' said Walt.

The doctor just stared at the body of Frank Allen.

Walt stepped back a pace from the slumped figure and withdrew the papers from inside his jacket. He glanced down at the name on the papers, then said in a voice of authority, 'Francis William Allen, I am US Deputy Marshal Walter Douglas Garfield and I hereby serve you with a warrant for your arrest on crimes as subscribed in these here papers.'

The doctor sat rigidly perched on the little bench, his eyes still fixed, unblinking, on Frank.

'I now serve you with these papers and you are to come with me, peaceably.' Walt tossed a document tied with a ribbon on to Frank's lap only to see it slide down between his legs and fall to the floor.

'Your refusal,' continued Walt, 'not to

accept this summons and to accompany me will be seen as a refusal. What say you?'

The silence hung like the cold chill of death that had taken Frank from this world.

Walt pulled his new Smith & Wesson pistol from its belt holster and cocked the action. The sound of each mechanical click jerked the doctor's head like a string puppet.

'What say you, I said?'

Walt pointed his handgun at Frank.

'Your refusal to respond leaves me with no other choice, Frank. You are resisting arrest.'

It was the final ultimatum from Walt just before he squeezed the trigger.

8

Telegrams

Sunday 7 to Thursday 11 August
Walt's telegram, advising of Frank's death and requesting additional funds for the burial and other expenses, reached James P. Everette some two days later. This delay was beyond Walt's control as the telegraph office was closed on Sunday, which was the day following Frank's departure from this world.

In fact, everything in Atoka was closed on Sunday except for the church and the undertaker. The church was commemorating the Confirmation and Endowment of the Holy Spirit, while the undertaker was preparing and dressing Frank's body for its final journey.

Walt had not seen the inside of a

church in years and wasn't about to break the habit, but he did have to become involved in the arrangements for the funeral by paying the undertaker a deposit of twenty-five dollars.

He then went back to the hotel and, as a house guest, was able to purchase liquor on the Sabbath, which he did, and got drunk.

When Everette received and read the telegram sent by Walt it was with astonishment and excitement. In just one week, from recruitment and selection, this new deputy marshal had achieved the first of the three goals that had been set for him. Such success was beyond Marshal Everette's wildest expectations as he ecstatically telegraphed his superior.

Marshal John Sims, who had now returned to Fort Smith, was similarly enthusiastic at such a speedy result and sent a telegram to Benjamin Bristow, the solicitor-general of the newly formed Department of Justice in Washington, advising that Frank Allen, a vicious and violent criminal responsible for lawlessness and the death of a federal officer, had been killed while being taken into custody in the Indian Territory.

Solicitor-General Bristow passed the telegram to his deputy solicitor-general, who acted with haste by sending two officers to Capitol Hill to inform members of the Senate and the House of Representatives of the news. Senator Joseph Cater Abbott, Republican from North Carolina, said that it was a demonstration of law and order being upheld in even the most remote parts of the nation.

The deputy solicitor-general then sent a telegram to his personal friend, Louis Jennings, the editor of the *New York Times*, seeking his assistance in publicizing the story. Jennings, who saw law and order as important public issues, responded as follows by return telegram:

SENDING TO YOU A CORRESPONDENT TO FOLLOW UP ON YOUR

GOOD WORK. PLEASE FACILITATE HIS JOURNEY INTO THE FIELD SO THAT HE MAY REPORT ON ANY FUTURE UNFOLDING EVENTS.

Walt was completely oblivious to all these political proceedings. He attended Frank's funeral on Wednesday and on Thursday morning when he awoke he had half a mind to take off to Henrietta without paying either the doctor his reward or the undertaker the remainder of his bill. However, he fell back into a deep sleep, having had a hard night on the whiskey, and did not wake again till noon.

When he did resurface from his comatose slumber it was because of the hefty banging against the door of his hotel room. It was the telegraph clerk. In his hand he held the reply telegram from Everette. It read:

STAY PUT. ADDITIONAL FUNDS AS REQUESTED ON WAY WITH A COURIER FROM NEW YORK NAMED

LUNDY. ALL WILL BE EXPLAINED
ON HIS ARRIVAL. PLEASE GIVE ALL
NECESSARY ASSISTANCE.

Walt thought this was most impressive.

'Fancy,' he mumbled to himself, 'sending a courier all the way from New York with my money. I wonder if I should have asked for more?' He then went back to sleep for another hour before washing up and wandering downstairs to the bar.

When he told Bert, the Atoka hotelkeeper, that he would be staying until further notice he was greeted by a broad smile and told that his first drink was on the house.

Walt smiled back and said, 'Well then, let's set 'em up.'

9

Newsworthy

Friday 19 August

'So you're not a courier?' Walt was leaning against the bar and his intake of whiskey was starting to show in his belligerent manner.

'No,' said the respectful young man in his city suit and vest.

'But you were sent with my money?'

'I was given the money by Marshal Sims at Fort Smith on my way to you. He said that it had been couriered up from Fort Worth, and that I was to pass it to you personally. It was sealed in this same envelope when it was given to me.'

Walt took the envelope and glanced at the cover with his name and title.

'But you've come by railroad from New York to Washington, then to

Memphis, and by coach to Fort Smith and then to Atoka, to deliver it to me?'

'Ahh . . . yes . . . no.'

'Yes, no, what?' said Walt. He broke the seal on the flap, lifted out the notes part way and ran his thumb over the edge to fan them, twice.

The neat man gripped at his straw hat with its blue ribbon tied around the crown and drew in a breath.

'I've come to report on you to our nation. I'm a correspondent from the *New York Times*.'

Walt's eyes half closed to make him look like a sullen reptile ready to bite.

'Why would I need to be reported on by a correspondent from the *New York Times*?'

'Because my editor says so.' Then the young man added, 'And so did the solicitor-general in Washington, and Marshal Sims at Fort Smith. They all said that you are newsworthy.'

'Newsworthy? What sort of bull is that?' Walt was loud and the other patrons in the saloon turned to look at him.

'I just assumed that you would be pleased to see me.'

Walt realized that maybe he was making a spectacle of himself and lowered his voice.

'With my money, yes, but not this newsworthy bunkum. What did you say your name was, again?'

'Lundy. William Lundy.'

'Bill, thanks for bringing the money, but I'm leaving for Henrietta in the morning so you've just run out of time to make me newsworthy. I've been held up here for too long already, waiting, and it's costing me time and expense. Hotels don't come cheap. And why you had to deliver my money from Fort Smith, personally, when they could have put it on a coach and had it here in three days is beyond me.'

'Where's Henrietta?'

'What?'

'Where's Henrietta?'

'Texas.'

'You're leaving the Territory? But I've

been assigned to travel with you on your journey through the Indian Territory as you dispense justice. We need to stay in the Indian Territory.'

'What?'

'You and me. I've been assigned — '

'No,' cut in Walt. 'The dispensing justice bit? You said that I dispense justice.'

'It was what I was told you were doing.'

Walt squinted at Lundy. 'What else have you been told?'

'To report on situations where law and order are restored, and on your life as a US deputy marshal.'

'Well, that ain't going to happen.'

Lundy looked shocked. 'Don't you want the fame that will follow?'

'Nope.' Walt poured a drink from the whiskey bottle and the glass nearly overflowed.

'Or the fortune?'

Walt stopped abruptly and his eyes narrowed.

'What fortune?'

'Being a public luminary often brings with it a financial reward.'

Walt fixed his gaze on the young man.

'How much?'

'It depends. We recently reported on the exploits of William Cody, the scout of the Fifth Cavalry regiment.'

'The scout?' queried Walt, emphasizing the word *the*. 'I'm sure they have more than one.'

William Lundy seemed not to hear Walt's mockery.

'He was instrumental in the victory over the savage Cheyenne.'

'So the Cheyenne are savage, eh? I thought we did a fair job of that during the war.'

Once again Lundy seemed not to hear.

'His stories have made him a personage of great public affection, and have led to appearances on the stage, for which he is handsomely paid. And then there is General George Custer. He is also an Indian fighter, and has killed over one hundred Cheyenne warriors.'

'Wonder there are any Cheyenne left at the rate these personages of affection are claiming victory,' mocked Walt.

'Then there is the champagne.'

Walt's chin immediately lifted to point at Lundy.

'French champagne?'

'Yes, they all drink French champagne.'

'Cody and Custer?'

'Of course. Have you tried it?'

'Yes, I've tried it.'

'Did you like it?'

'Yes, I liked it.'

'I believe it's expensive,' said Lundy.

'Yes, along with the company it keeps.'

'I'm here to service the readers of the *New York Times*, but in doing so I will also be servicing your reputation and position in our nation.'

Walt looked unimpressed. 'Have you got a horse?'

'No, sir.'

'Provisions?'

'No, sir.'

'Money?'

'I was advanced two hundred and fifty dollars for expenses. It has cost me over forty dollars already in transportation, accommodation and meals just to get here. I had no idea it was going to be so expensive, or this far.'

Walt was now interested. 'Can you ride?'

'Of course. I ride around Central Park most Sundays, except in winter.'

'How dandy.' Walt poured another drink.

'I will have to purchase a horse.'

'Well, there goes at least one hundred and thirty dollars, and that's for a horse of modest stamina with a stiff ride-saddle thrown in. Then there are your provisions. You'll need to spend eight dollars a week on necessities, and on this trip I expect to be riding for weeks. So I guess that inside a month you'll not have enough left for the cost of a ticket home.'

'I've been told to keep an account, and that all reasonable expenses will be reimbursed.'

'I see,' said Walt. 'So your boss is keen to pick up the tab, is he?'

'Most definitely, and the new Department of Justice is to assist.'

Walt tilted his head in thought. 'I can rent you a horse and provide provisions for four dollars and fifty cents a day. You'll need to buy a top blanket and a soft saddle, not new, and that'll cost you thirty, maybe forty dollars out here. What sort of gun do you carry? I have some ammunition, at a price.'

'I don't carry a gun.'

'You don't? What do you carry, then?'

'My writing implements: ink, pens, paper and pencils. All portable.'

'I mean, what do you carry to protect yourself from attack?'

'Nothing.'

'So your newspaper boss and the new department expects me to protect you as well?'

'Well, you are a lawman. A US

deputy marshal.'

The reminder of his appointment made Walt feel a little sheepish. 'Yeah, OK. Let's call it five dollars a day all up.'

'I really didn't realize how costly this field trip would be,' said William Lundy. 'It was put together with such haste, but I guess it will be all right.'

'Don't let me put you on the spot. None of this is my idea. I'm just trying to make it work.'

'No, of course, I agree, five dollars a day, starting from tomorrow,' said Lundy and held out his hand.

Walt put down his glass and took Lundy's hand.

As they shook Lundy said, 'Now you must tell me about the shooting of Frank Allen and introduce me to any witnesses.'

Walt went silent, and even though he'd been imbibing for most of the afternoon he now felt like he needed another drink.

10

A Professional Man

Saturday 20 August

Walt had woken with a hangover headache. It had come from a self-inflicted injury that left him with that familiar feeling of remorse that repentant drunks know so well. He knew that the bottle had got the better of him once again, and the consequences had landed him in a terrible bind. William Lundy had nagged him to the point where he had relented, in a moment of weakness, and promised to introduce him to the doctor, so that he could conduct an eyewitness interview on the killing of Frank Allen.

The cold hard light of day had now arrived, and with it the realization that he could be unmasked as a man — no, as a US deputy marshal — who had shot a corpse sitting in a chair. Then there would be the legal matters of claiming the reward and fiddling with the certificate of death. How could any of this be explained if the truth was to come out? It was enough to turn a man to drink, thought Walt, when he caught sight of William Lundy hurrying down the hotel stairs to breakfast.

'As soon as we eat can we see the doctor?' The words raced from the lips of the *New York Times* reporter with youthful enthusiasm.

'You eat. I'll go down and see the doctor; then you can follow after your breakfast. His chamber is just down the street, with a sign hanging out front.'

When Walt arrived at the doctor's he found a chalked slate hanging from a rope on the doorhandle, saying *back in 5*. He waited for ten minutes before the doctor arrived.

'I've got your money,' said Walt as a terse welcome.

The doctor glanced around quickly and said under his breath, 'Best you come inside, we don't want anyone to hear.'

Walt counted the money out on to a small side table, but before the doctor could lay a finger upon his earnings Walt snatched the notes back up and made his proposition.

'I've been saddled with a newspaperman who wants to speak to you about the killing.'

'Newspaperman?' repeated the doctor with concern. 'I can't talk to a newspaperman.'

'All you have to do is tell him what you saw me do and say it real simple. It will only take a minute or two.' Then Walt added, 'You have no choice.'

'I sure do,' said the doctor. 'My choice is I won't do it.'

Walt fanned the notes close to the doctor's face. 'Then you won't get a penny of this.'

The doctor paused, then said quickly, 'I earned that money. I wrote out the certificate of death.'

'Yep, you did. You forged a legal

document for money.'

The doctor instantly looked ill, as if he had eaten a bad oyster. 'But I haven't got my money, yet.'

'And you're not going to unless you talk to Lundy.'

'I knew I shouldn't have done it. I knew I shouldn't have got involved with people like you and Frank.'

Walt took offence. 'Like me and Frank?'

'Yes,' said the doctor. 'You are one and the same.'

Walt was incensed. 'If I'm like Frank, then you're like me. This is the situation and we need to make the best of it. This money is yours, to do with what you want, but only if you speak to William Lundy and just tell him what you saw.'

'I saw you shoot a dead man.'

'Not that part, you idiot. Just the part where I served the papers and he refused to take them or accompany me. And maybe you could throw in that he looked like he was going for his gun.'

'Now lies,' said the doctor. 'This is very risky.'

'It will only be risky if you don't talk to this reporter. It will raise suspicion.'

'What if I don't?' The doctor was being defiant and he stuck out his chin as if to challenge Walt to strike it.

'If you don't,' said Walt, waving the notes around, 'first, you won't get this money. I'll keep it. Second, I'll say you were a willing party as demonstrated by your forgery of the death certificate.'

'You could have threatened me,' said the doctor in protest. 'I could have signed it under duress.'

'Won't wash,' said Walt. 'You filled out the whole form and your handwriting is neat and clear. And third, I will give you the biggest pistol-whipping you've ever had in your life.'

'You'd do that to me, an educated physician, a professional man who has dedicated his life to the health and hygiene of others?'

'It's not my first choice, but if you are unreasonable, then you leave me with nowhere else to go.'

The doctor thought for a moment or two, shaking his head. Then he looked up and said, 'You will have to pay me more. If I am going to do this, then it only seems reasonable that I receive some additional remuneration.'

'You're already getting two fifty.'

'What about the turban-heads you've got on you?'

'What turban-heads?' said Walt.

'You gave one to McBride the night you arrived.'

'Who told you that?'

'McBride. He told you where to find Frank, didn't he?'

'Geezes,' said Walt. 'I gave him that coin to keep his trap shut.'

'No, you didn't. He said that you paid him to keep quiet over a man you were asking about by the name of Taylor.'

'Geezes, what is it with this town? Can't anyone keep a secret?'

'I can,' said the doctor, 'but it's going to cost you.'

A loud knocking came from the front of the passage, rattling the glass in the door. It was then followed by a call from William Lundy to see if anyone was home.

'OK,' whispered Walt. 'I'll throw in a turban-head.'

'Two,' said the doctor in return.

'Two? This is daylight robbery.'

Lundy banged on the door and called again.

Walt relented. 'OK, two,' but from his tone it was clear that he wasn't happy.

'Now,' said the doctor, 'before he comes in.'

Walt handed over the notes and withdrew one gold piece from his top shirt pocket and a second from the buttoned pocket of his trousers.

The doctor quickly tucked the paper money into his jacket, examined the two gold coins, then dropped them into his vest pocket as he took in a breath and called out in a cheery voice, 'Come on in, it's open.'

11

Look Up

Sunday 21 to Tuesday 23 August

'I'm exhilarated,' said William Lundy. 'I have an independent eyewitness account of your gallant actions in apprehending a violent criminal, and have filed my first report by telegraph. And now, I am riding the range with a US deputy marshal, under the western sun in a landscape of wonder.'

'It's morning. The sun is still in the east,' corrected Walt. 'And I wouldn't get too carried away with all the wonder if I were you. The only thing out here is grass, mesquite and cactus, and it's going to get hot.'

William would have none of Walt's pessimism. He was a man of enthusiasm and elation and it showed on his face.

Walt took a moment to observe the young reporter and concluded that he just looked smug and silly in his small straw hat with its blue ribbon fluttering in the breeze.

'Hurry up,' he called. 'We have one hundred and fifty miles to go and I want to be there the day after tomorrow.'

★　★　★

When they did arrive in Henrietta, at sundown on the third day, William Lundy's sunburnt face now showed disappointment. The hard ride had left him so saddle-sore he could hardly walk, and what he had imagined in his mind's eye to be a neat and thriving town looked, in the fading light, to be more like ancient ruins from a biblical tale. Old tumbledown and burnt-out mud brick buildings indicated past failures to establish a township.

What had grown up instead was a sprawling tent city formed of clusters of smaller settlements. It was scattered, untidy, and with no sense of permanency, while the inhabitants seemed scrawny and miserable. It would have made William feel like he had arrived at the ends of the earth had it not been for the small wooden sign marking the telegraph station, which was also situated inside a tent.

This small and temporary structure, with its thin copper wire running from Gainesville over sixty miles away to the east, represented a fragile link to his far-off world of city bustle, polished black carriages, glowing gas lamps, and a civilized Sunday stroll in Central Park. These thoughts of home made him feel alone and abandoned.

His glum mood was made worse when Walt left William with the horses and their provisions in a rough makeshift camp on open ground, just a short walk from the saloon.

'I'll be back,' was all he said as he walked off.

Called the Texas Top, the saloon was

a makeshift affair constructed from sailcloth stretched over half a dozen tent poles and tied down to two wagons, one on each side. The interior was expansive but crowded, and the dust from stomping feet upon the bare ground was made to glint in the air by the light of the oil lamps. When Walt eventually got served, the whiskey was raw and expensive. He winced when he took his first sip, then asked, 'What is this?'

'Are you complaining?' accused the bartender with menace.

Walt looked up at the giant of a man, whose head nearly touched the canvas roof.

'Not me,' he said, smiling, and quickly changed the subject. 'I just got in from Atoka and I'm looking for some people. Firstly, a man by the name of Taylor, Jason Taylor. He's travelling with a Mexican woman. Then second, a man by the name of Louis Bolan. Then third — '

The bartender cut Walt short, his

face stern and his stare cold.

'In this town we don't ask about who's here; who's been here, or who's coming here. Got it?'

'Got it,' said Walt. He looked around to see if there was anyone else he could talk to. The customers were a mix of Indian traders, buffalo-hunters and cattlemen. Few of the migrating settlers had been enticed from their wagons or tents to taste the rotgut that was being served as whiskey.

'You want another drink?' asked the bartender.

'No, I'll sit on this one,' said Walt as he tried to engage with a smile, but it didn't work.

A voice close by said, 'It tastes like cat's piss, don't it? But it does get better after a while. You've just got to persevere.' The statement was followed by a cackle of high-pitched laughter.

Walt turned to see a smallish old man with some missing teeth and a full beard. He was wearing a well-worn hide jacket that showed his trade as a buffalo-hunter, but it was his eyes that caught Walt's attention. They were sky blue and could have belonged to a younger man.

'Could start a drinker to think of abstinence,' said Walt, to make conversation.

'Gets you in the throat, doesn't it, just like an eagle's claw?' The old hunter's eyes smiled as he edged in a little. 'See Big John gave you advice to mind your own business in Henrietta.'

'Friendly place,' said Walt.

'It's good advice, though. People keep to themselves because they have things that they need to keep to themselves, if you get what I mean.'

Walt nodded that he understood.

'If you are looking for someone you are going to have to search for them yourself, but if people don't know who you are, then they tend to clam up.'

'I'll keep that in mind.'

'I could keep my ear to the ground, for a price. I heard those names you are looking for. Taylor and Bolan.'

'You've got good hearing,' said Walt. He finished his drink in one gulp and pressed his lips tight to stop from choking.

'The name's Ned.'

Walt went to say 'Who?' but could only mouth the word.

'Ned,' repeated the old man.

Walt nodded, still unable to get a word out. He made his way to leave, Ned following. Just as Walt pulled back the flap to let himself out he heard the shouts of a commotion off to the left. It was from a large group of people standing close to a community fire, watching what seemed to be a confrontation. He was about to walk on when he saw from the flashes of firelight that one of the spectators was Lundy.

'Geezes,' he said under his breath, and made his way over to the reporter. Ned continued to follow.

'What are you doing here?' said Walt, annoyed. 'Who's guarding our outfit and supplies?'

'I came to see what was going on. A

woman is being maliciously ill-treated.'

Walt glanced over the heads of the onlookers and could see a woman, very upset, with tear tracks glistening on her cheeks. While he could hear the shouts, he was unable to understand what was being said.

'Nothing to do with me,' he said. 'I'm going to bed.'

A woman next to Lundy yelled out, 'Leave her alone, you brute.' Some other women close by joined in, calling out, 'Brute, brute, brute.'

'Why doesn't someone stop him?' said William Lundy. 'She is being beaten and humiliated.'

The woman next to Lundy answered: 'Because there are no real men here. No gentlemen and no law.'

'But the law is here,' said Lundy. 'Deputy Marshal Garfield is here.'

'Where?' asked the woman.

'Here,' said Lundy pointing to Walt.

Walt had turned to leave.

'Help her, Marshal,' called the woman. 'You've got to help her. This has happened before and one day he'll kill her.'

Walt threw a condemning glance at Lundy, then reluctantly stopped, turned and took in a long breath before making his way slowly through the crowd. In the centre, near the fire, he could see a strong and belligerent young man laying down the law to a heavily pregnant young woman. Dirt was upon her clothes and face where she had fallen or been pushed to the ground. Walt could only hear snippets of what was being said by the man, but he caught the gist from the profanities being voiced.

Walt stopped and called to the crowd. 'Come on, move along, time for everyone to go home.'

Some in the crowd let out a jeer of disapproval.

Walt called to the man, 'And leave that gal alone.'

The man turned towards Walt, his face showing his rage and aggression.

'Who are you?'

'He's a US marshal,' called the woman standing alongside William Lundy.

'You have no right, she's my wife.'

'Then take her home and sort out your differences there,' said Walt. This comment caused the crowd to jeer again, but this time it was the women, and Walt half-turned his head to see their reaction.

'I ain't taking this bitch anywhere, she needs a good public scolding, and I'm going to give it to her.'

'Why?' asked Walt. 'What can a girl this young, and one with child, do to deserve a public reprimand in front of her neighbours?'

'That's my business.'

'No, it's not,' said Walt. 'You've made it everybody's business now.'

A cheer erupted from the crowd.

'Back off,' said the husband. He grabbed a handful of his wife's hair and gave a yank that caused her to spin around and stumble to the ground, shedding more tears.

'Are you armed?' asked Walt.

'What?' shouted the husband.

'I said, are you armed? Are you carrying a gun?'

'No,' said the man, a little confused.

'Geezes,' said Walt. 'It would have been so much easier if you had been.' He pulled on the buckle of his gunbelt and called out. 'Bill Lundy, get here.'

Lundy squeezed through the crowd.

'Hold this,' said Walt, his outstretched hand clutching his rig.

Lundy took the belt and was surprised at its weight.

Walt strode forward. 'Look up,' he called to the woman's hostile husband. He pointed to the heavens with an outstretched right arm and a finger directed at the stars.

The husband, bewildered for a moment, glanced up just for a fraction of a second, but it was long enough for Walt to let fly with a tight left fist. It caught the bully on the side of his face with a loud whack that made the crowd gasp. The husband's head snapped back and, stumbling sideways, he fell to the ground.

The crowd cheered with appreciation. Walt turned to accept their applause just as a return fist hit the back of his head and sent him sprawling.

He quickly scrambled to his feet, only to be knocked to the ground again by a shoulder, which hit him in the ribs. Frantically he rolled to the side as he narrowly evaded the toe of a fast boot, which flew past his face. Walt rolled over again, just in time to see the dark figure above him advance. While still on the ground he kicked out his boot, striking his opponent's ankle. It was a lucky blow and he knew it, but it sent his foe to the ground.

That gave Walt all the time he needed. He was on his feet, mustering his strength to launch himself towards the face-up figure upon the ground, to seize the opportunity that now presented itself. He stomped his boot on to his adversary's neck and pressed hard.

'Bill Lundy,' he called between deep breaths.

Lundy ran to Walt's side.

'My gunbelt.'

Bill thrust it forward. Walt drew the Smith & Wesson from the holster, pulled back on the hammer and pointed it at the husband's head.

'Ma'am,' he called to the wife, who was still upon the ground, half-sitting and in tears. 'Do you want to start all over again? Cos I can kill him now, which might be the best for everyone.'

The wife mouthed some words but nothing came out.

Walt looked down at the husband, whose eyes were showing fear as he stared up at the end of the .44's barrel.

'You wanted public,' said Walt. 'So, I'll give you public. All those in favour that I should shoot this son of a bitch, raise your hand.' As Walt kept his gun sighted, he called. 'You count, Bill.'

Lundy looked around. Most of the women had lifted their hands.

'Now, all those against?'

This time most of the men put their hands up.

'Looks about even, Marshal,' said Lundy.

'It's back to you, ma'am. What do you say? Let him live or die?'

Tears continued to stream down her cheeks and she stumbled over her words, which Walt couldn't hear.

'What was that?'

'Let him live,' she said, a little louder.

'OK,' said Walt. He lowered his aim slowly. 'But you have my permission to shoot your husband in his sleep if he ever does this to you again. These folk here tonight are your witnesses to the approval I have given to you. Do you understand?'

The wife slowly got to her feet and nodded. 'Yes,' she said.

Then one woman, the one who had been standing next to Bill Lundy, began to clap her hands, politely at first, before the other onlookers joined her in a flurry, including Bill Lundy, who was the most exuberant in his applause.

12

Pride

Wednesday 24 August — Early Morning

'Why don't you wear your badge?' asked Ned.

William Lundy followed like an echo. 'Why don't you, Marshal?'

'It's Walt,' he replied, showing his annoyance with the inquisition.

Ned and Bill Lundy waited in silence for Walt to answer their question.

Walt finally relented. 'Because I don't want to draw attention to myself.'

'You did that last night,' said Ned. 'Not everyone in Henrietta may know you by sight, but they all know you by name and reputation. We haven't seen such sport in months.'

'I don't want to scare away the

people I'm looking for,' said Walt in self-defence.

'Too late,' said Ned. 'You told their names to Big John, so that will also be all over the settlement by now. Word travels like wildfire here.' Ned looked over at William Lundy. 'We don't have a newspaper, so that's how we get to know what's going on, see.'

'Going on?' scoffed Walt. 'More like gossiping on, if you ask me.'

'If you were to wear your badge then you'd find out more,' said Ned.

'Yeah? How do you figure that?' ridiculed Walt.

'People become respectful.'

Walt was getting fed up with the conversation and threw the dregs of his coffee to sizzle in the small fire in their makeshift camp. Then he said sarcastically: 'Oh yeah, so who in particular is going to be respectful?'

'After last night, the women, of course,' cackled Ned, showing the gap made by a missing tooth. Then he added, 'And with your badge on, the women will tell you what they know. And believe me, they always know.'

William Lundy joined in. 'Ned could be right. In New York the police often interview women for information on the whereabouts of criminals.'

Walt grunted.

'Can I at least see your badge?' asked William.

Walt grunted again.

'It's in his saddle wallet,' said Ned.

Walt looked up at Ned. 'How did you know that?'

'I saw it when I was cleaning up the camp.'

'What, inside my valise?'

'It dropped out, sort of.'

'I'm paying you to keep an eye on things when I'm away, not to go riffling through them.'

'I'm no thief,' said Ned. 'Besides, you've got nothing I want.'

'Except my money,' said Walt.

'Only what you pay me, fair and square.'

'Can I see?' said Lundy.

'What?' snapped Walt.

'Your badge?'

'I'll get it,' said Ned. He pushed himself to his feet and shuffled over to the side of their little camp where the stores were stacked under a canvas sheet. When he returned he handed the badge to William Lundy, not Walt.

William took it gently in his hand and gazed upon the emblem of authority.

Walt was just about to say, *it's just a piece of metal*, when he caught the look of respect in Lundy's eyes as he carefully examined the badge and caressed the smooth metal surface with his fingers.

'Put it on,' said the young reporter. 'You should be proud to wear this.'

'And why is that?' asked Walt.

'Because it represents the rule of law for all in our nation. It identifies you as a protector, just like you were last night when you helped that poor unfortunate woman. You defended the defenceless, and you were fearless.'

'Give it here,' said Walt as he thrust out his hand. 'Defended the defenceless? Fearless? Let me tell you that there is no such thing as fearless, and anyone who tells you different is either a liar or a fool,' he stated.

But as he pinned the badge on to his jacket something happened that surprised him. He glanced down at the five-pointed star in the centre of the crescent and read the inscription: Deputy United States Marshal. He felt an immediate sensation of lightness, a little like floating, that seemed to invigorate and give strength. It was an odd feeling and certainly not at all unpleasant. He wondered what it could be. Then the uncomfortable thought flashed through his mind. *Is it pride?*

13

Rose's Doves

Same Day — Late Morning
'Marshal.'

Walt felt the tug on his coat sleeve and turned to see a woman standing behind him, her blue-and-white cotton bonnet pulled low to hide her eyes, before she looked up.

William Lundy smiled and removed his straw hat, immediately recognizing her as the woman who had been standing next to him just the night before at the fight. Her voice had been strident when she called out to Walt, but now she spoke softly. 'I've heard that you are looking for people.'

Walt nodded politely but said nothing.

She glanced around as if to see that no one was listening. 'Then best you speak to the girls.'

'That's what I've been doing, ma'am,' said Walt. 'But with little luck.'

'No,' she corrected, putting a finger to her lips. 'You need to talk to the calico girls.'

William was confused, but Walt wasn't. 'Oh, I see, those girls.'

William went to ask who were the calico girls, only to receive a dig in the ribs from Walt's elbow.

'And could you direct me to where I need to go to speak to . . . ' he lowered his voice, 'them?'

'Down by the creek.'

'Anyone in particular?' asked Walt.

'Rose. She looks after the girls. Speak to her.'

Walt lifted his hat in appreciation, while William felt obliged to wave his around in his hand as if to confirm that it was off his head.

'What's a calico girl?' asked William when the woman was out of earshot.

'A dove.'

William was none the wiser.

'Soiled dove,' said Walt. 'Painted cat, sporting woman, lady of the night.'

William finally got it. 'They have them here?'

Walt stopped. 'Why not here?' he asked with a touch of irritation. 'Is only New York City allowed to have any fun?'

'I just thought that, you know, way out here . . . ' William Lundy was getting flustered and searching for words.

Walt started walking. 'What does way out here have to do with anything? Do you think urges change over distance? My experience is that they get stronger.' Walt stopped again and looked at William. 'Bill, have you ever had anything to do with these gals?'

'Oh, no,' said Lundy. 'Never.'

'Don't be so smug,' said Walt. 'You might just like it.' He then started to stride off, only to realize that Lundy wasn't with him. He stopped and turned back to look at the young newspaperman. 'Are you coming?'

'Oh, I don't think so,' said William. 'I couldn't.'

Walt started off again, saying to himself, *And you call yourself a newspaper reporter.*

William Lundy decided to follow in quick steps that seemed to keep him a little out of breath.

'But I couldn't report on them, my editor wouldn't allow it.'

'Suit yourself,' said Walt.

'Although I could think of it as an enquiry into the ways of the West.'

Walt lifted his eyebrows. 'Don't you mean the ways of the world? Could also give the girls a chance to enquire into you, too.'

'Me? Why would they be interested in me?'

Walt stopped and turned front-on to William Lundy.

'Bill, are you interested in girls?'

William stumbled over some words but Walt knew the answer.

'Well then, why is it so hard to understand that girls might be interested in you?'

William looked stunned.

Walt turned and started walking. When they passed a row of settlers' tents on the way to the creek women appeared and called a morning greeting to Walt, along with his title of 'Marshal'. They then smiled at William, whose cheeks were flushed with concern that they knew where he was heading.

At the creek Walt asked a trader where he might find Rose. The stocky man, with sleeves rolled up, was in the middle of repairs to his wagon, which he had emptied of all its stock so that the axle could be lifted up on to a water barrel and the wheel removed. He was bent over the wheel-hub and applying grease, but he pointed his blackened hand towards a group of tents some two hundred yards away.

Walt thanked him and said, 'Broke, eh?'

'Fixed now, but it's too late. I was expecting to head up north tomorrow, but the train I was going to travel with left early this morning.'

'How long will you have to wait?'

asked Walt, just to make conversation.

'Week, maybe more.'

'Why don't you just follow up behind?'

'On my own?'

'Just till you catch up,' said Walt.

'Till I lose my scalp,' said the trader. 'You won't get me going into Indian country without an armed escort.'

'But we did, just the two of us, from Atoka,' said William.

The trader looked at Walt's badge, then across to Lundy. 'You were travelling with a US marshal and I bet you were on horseback, not creaking along in a wagon. I can't outrun Indians in this and I'm no gunman. I'm a merchant.'

William felt foolish, so said nothing and left with hurried footsteps to catch up with Walt as he strode towards the cluster of tents.

When they found Rose they were met with a strong European accent and striking dark eyes. Although some dozen or more years older that Walt, she still held her charms, along with a precocious manner.

'I know all about you,' she said. 'You are a fighter, so ask me anything.' Then she said, 'I am also no shrinking lily myself.'

'Violet,' corrected William Lundy quietly.

'Who are you?' she snapped, but before William could answer she said, 'Your hat is a ridicule.'

'Don't you mean ridiculous?'

'That too,' she quipped, then turned her attention back to Walt with a smile.

'Why don't you go for a look around,' said Walt to William. 'While Rose and I talk.'

'On my own?'

'They won't bite you.'

'Well, I hope not,' laughed Rose. Then she called out, 'Pearl, Pearl darling, come and show this boy around and don't bite on him.'

A young lady called back, then appeared from behind a curtain hung across the back of the tent. She was still fixing her hair, which was piled high to expose a pretty round face and long neck. She smiled and William blushed.

Walt waited a little, until William Lundy's back was turned, then he asked, 'Do you know of a man called Taylor? Jason Taylor?'

Rose shook her head.

'He is travelling with a Mexican woman. Younger than him.'

'Is she pretty?' asked Rose.

Walt hesitated, then reluctantly said, 'Yeah, she's pretty all right.'

'Then he would have no need to meet with me or my girls. But for you I will ask around.'

'The other men I am looking for are a Frenchy called Louis Bolan and a Mexican called Cobos, Eloy Cobos.'

'Is the Mexican and the woman, together?'

'No,' said Walt. 'The woman is with Taylor.'

'But they have both come from Mexico?'

'Yes, but they are not associated.'

'No matter,' said Rose. 'I haven't seen any Mexicans and I don't know of any man called Taylor. But I know of Monsieur Bolan. Some of his men have been here.'

'When?'

'Last time?'

'Yes.'

'Two, maybe three days ago.'

'Are you sure?'

'Sure I'm sure. I have to see him for payment. One of his men cheats on one of my girls and underpays. I tell him no payment, then no poky for anyone in his camp. So he gets me my pay.'

'Where is Bolan now?'

'Over there.' Rose pointed over to where Walt had come from.

'How many men does he have with him?'

'Five, maybe six. Maybe more, I'm not sure.'

'If you hear of Taylor, will you let me know?' Walt said, digging into the pocket of his trousers.

'You only pay me if I find out, OK?'

'OK,' said Walt. Then he called, 'Bill Lundy, let's go.'

'Oh,' said Rose, pulling a face of concern. 'Now you go and spoil a young man's fancy.'

'Just tell him I've gone, he can — '

'Follow after you,' said Rose. 'When he is all finished up.'

Walt pulled on the brim of his hat in appreciation, then turned and walked towards where Rose had pointed. When he passed the trader, who was readying to put the wagon wheel back on to the axle, he stopped to give him a hand.

'Easier with two,' said the trader, 'but I could have managed.'

'Sure you could,' said Walt, looking around. Then he said quietly, 'Do you know of a Frenchman named Bolan? Louis Bolan?'

'Yes, I know him.' The response was given with a hint of distaste.

'Where might I find him?'

'Not here. He left this morning. He was in charge of the train that I was supposed to travel with. He just took off out of the blue. We were supposed to leave tomorrow.'

'So did he leave on his own?'

'Hell no! He left with everyone else except me, just before first light. What the damn hurry was I still don't know. Less than half a day is all I needed for repairs and now I'll have to wait at least a week.'

'Where are they heading?'

'North for the settlers. One couple are heading for the Santa Fe Trail, so they will then go west.'

'West where?'

'On the Spanish Trail. They are going right through to California.'

'California,' said Walt slowly, then fell silent.

The trader waited for him to continue, to say something, but still Walt remained mute, until at last he said carefully, 'By chance, was that man around my height, a little heavier and older?'

The trader nodded.

'Was he travelling with a younger woman?'

The trader nodded again.

'Mexican?'

'Mexican? I thought Louisiana Creole. Mind you, I never spoke to her, direct. He did all the talking and buying, and that's when he said they had come from New Orleans and were heading for California. Seems he was an argonaut and did the same journey around '49.' The trader wiped his hands on a rag, then dropped it next to the grease bucket.

'His name is — '

'I know his name. It's Taylor. Jason Taylor.'

'That's right. Are you looking for him, Marshal?'

'Yeah, I'm looking for both of them.'

'Are you going after them?'

But Walt didn't answer; he had already turned and was striding back up the road towards his camp.

14

Lovesick and Saddle-Sore

Same Day — Early Afternoon

'Are we leaving?'

'I am,' said Walt, without looking at William Lundy, as he packed up the camp stores.

'Where are we going?'

'I am going north, back into the Indian Territory to chase down a wanted man.'

'You know where to find him?'

'He left here about eight hours ago, so he has the jump on us. But I'd expect to catch up by the day after tomorrow, if we hurry along and don't lose their tracks.'

'So this man is not on his own?'

'Nope, he has company.'

'To protect him? Will you be in danger?'

'Maybe, but Ned is coming along.' Then he added, 'At a price.'

William looked around. 'Where is he?'

'He's gone to get his horse and rifle. I've got a spare pistol for you, if you're coming along, so that will make three of us, and that should be enough. If we all shoot straight.'

'I'm a reporter, not a gunman.'

'Then you'll have to learn as you go.'

'What a day,' said Lundy.

'What was that?' said Walt. He pulled on the cinch then threaded the buckle.

'I just said, I have had a day.'

'I expect you have and it isn't finished yet, so load up, if you are with us.'

'Are you young Will?'

William Lundy looked around, but had to squint on account of the brightness of the sun before he could see Ned astride his horse with a large rifle resting across his lap.

'Three of us against how many others?' asked William.

'What? Altogether or just those who are armed and willing to fight?' asked Walt.

'Both.'

'Don't know, actually, but my guess is twenty to thirty in the first bunch and half a dozen to a dozen in the second.'

'And just three of us. We will be outnumbered.'

'That's mostly how it works, but such odds can be overcome.'

'How?' asked the young newspaper reporter.

'Oh, a little thought, some daring, and a whole lot of luck.'

'And that works?'

'Has for me,' said Walt, 'at least, up to now.'

★　★　★

The two days that followed were a mix of agony and enchantment for William Lundy. Agony, because the riding was hard, relentless and frustrating, as they were often forced to double back to re-find the unclear trail amongst the many other wagon tracks heading north. The enchantment came from dreamlike thoughts that constantly swirled around his head. He had been struck by Pearl's charms and just couldn't stop thinking about her skin, her lips, her kiss, and her touch; and all to the point of near distraction. When he nearly fell off his horse on one occasion, with a wistful expression on his face, Walt looked at him oddly, while Ned thought it was a hoot.

Old Ned, who moved stiff and slow when walking on his bowed legs, now seemed as agile as a young jockey when in the saddle. He was their scout, who examined the wagon tracks and lumps of dung left behind by the livestock of those they pursued. He seemed much sharper than William had given him initial credit for, as he was able to measure the gap in time that they were behind the wagon train, which they were closing. He also deduced that there were five wagons and between eight and a dozen riders accompanying the train and acting as protection to the flanks and rear. He concluded that the train was making good time as no one was on foot; instead, they were either mounted or on the wagons.

The route they were taking had started out almost due north, then slowly turned towards the west. This surprised William, who had thought that they would just continue north. When he quizzed Walt he got the sharp response that they were heading for the old overland trail.

'Why?' he asked.

'Because it goes to California,' mumbled Walt.

'Are they all going to California?' asked William.

'I know two that are.' There was a bitterness in Walt's response that took William by surprise.

'Are they the people you are after?'

But Walt would not elaborate. In fact, he wouldn't discuss the matter any further; instead he just seemed to withdraw into his own surly thoughts.

It was Ned who said to William, when Walt had gone to relieve himself and they were collecting up wood for the overnight campfire, 'They are making towards Santa Fe.'

'Who?'

'The people we are chasing after.'

'And who is it we are chasing after?'

'That's the marshal's business and he's not saying much. But I know who he was asking after in Henrietta.'

'Who?'

Ned leaned in close to William. 'A man named Taylor, a Mexican woman, and another man named Bolan. There is also a third man, but I didn't get to hear his name. Big John cut him short.'

'Who is Big John?'

'Runs the Henrietta saloon. The marshal was asking him if he knew them, but Big John told the marshal to clamp it.' Ned let out his familiar cackle.

'Why wouldn't he help the law?'

'A lot of men like Big John are not

out here by choice, they have a past and they don't want it to catch up with them, so they protect others in the hope that they get something in return.'

'So do you know why Marshal Garfield is after these people?'

'No,' said Ned.

'I should ask,' said William; his tone was that of a reporter with a duty.

'I wouldn't do that. If he had wanted you to know he would have told you. Best you just keep your ears open. That's what I do, and you learn all sorts of things.'

'Can you get to California this way?'

'Sure, this is the way some of the argonauts got to the gold-fields in '49 and '50,' said Ned. 'Was hard then but easier now, especially if you're Confederate. There are those right across New Mexico and Arizona Territory through to California that help their own kind, if needed.' Then Ned said, 'Did you see the Indians trailing us?'

'When?'

'Today. When we was riding west.'

'No,' said Lundy.

'They were watching us and would have seen you.' Ned winked at William.

'Me? Who were they?'

'Kiowas, I expect. Or it could be Arapahos.'

'Are they dangerous?'

'Depends what's on their mind.' Ned cackled and it was starting to get on William Lundy's nerves.

'Should we turn back?'

'Oh no,' said Ned firmly. 'While we are still going along they will want to watch, out of curiosity, but if we try going back, now, back to Henrietta, then they might think that we got scared.'

'Then what?'

'Then we become an easy target. We become their sport to ride down like they do to the buffalo.' Ned dropped his pile of firewood at his feet and glanced at the handgun tucked into William's trouser band. 'Do you know how to shoot that piece that the marshal gave you?'

'I've fired a handgun, once. We aimed at targets in the park.'

'Did you hit any?'

'Some.'

'That means you missed some too.'

'Some.'

'Miss too many and you'll be in trouble. So keep your eye on the target and your hand steady. If those Indians come after you, then you usually only get one chance.'

The old man smiled and placed the palm of his hand on top of his forehead, then grasped and pulled back a handful of grey hair. 'Before they take the trophy.'

William Lundy didn't say anything, but the look on his face was one of great unease.

15

Mercy

Saturday 27 August — Before Midday
It was Ned who saw the smoke first. It was just a wisp, low on the horizon, a little like a smudge on an otherwise clear sky.

'Campfire,' called William Lundy when he saw it.

Walt said nothing.

So William turned to Ned and repeated it again. 'It's a campfire.'

'No it's not,' said Ned.

'What is it, then?'

Ned glanced around, scanning the horizon.

'Ned, tell me. What is it? Is it a signal?'

'No signal, just trouble,' said Ned.

Walt rode in close. 'Bill, you take the two horses. Ned, you go to the left flank, I'll take up on the right. I want a spread of at least thirty yards between each of us. Bill, don't get in front; hang back a little, but not too far. Keep your eyes open and watch out for any surprises. It may be a trap. If it is, defend yourself first, then each other.'

William felt his stomach roll and he wanted to speak, to ask questions, but the look on Walt's face made it clear that this was not the time. So he took the halter of the lead packhorse from Walt and with a trembling hand fumbled a tie to the horn of his saddle.

As they advanced Walt waved them up to a trot, while William kept looking across to the left and right at each of his companions in the hope that he'd receive a sign that all was well. But what he saw were the straight backs of two alert men sitting tall in the saddle. In his mind's eye he now expected to be surprised at any moment by yelping savages descending upon him, but apart from the smoke that now swirled as a lazy haze before them, it was disturbingly peaceful.

When William saw Walt stand in the stirrups, then point over to the left, he turned just in time to see Ned wave back and charge his horse at the gallop. When he looked back to Walt he saw him turn sharply and bring his horse to the gallop as he yelled, 'Follow on.'

William Lundy pulled his horse to the left and dug in his heels, and in an instant his mouth went dry and his stomach rolled as he felt the fear start to grip. He had no idea what they were doing or why, and it was not until he smelt the pungent odour of the smoke, just as he came over a small rise, that he saw the carnage.

Before him, in a shallow depression devoid of vegetation, was the aftermath of a battle. A lone wagon, still smouldering, lay on its side where it had toppled when trying to turn sharply. The wheel ruts were clear and deep in the soft sand. To each side of this natural dip in the ground was an embankment upon which Walt and Ned now raced at a full gallop, and they did not stop until they were beyond by about one hundred yards. Only then did they turn back to ride directly into the hollow, still at a gallop.

William Lundy stopped the horses and just sat and looked at what was before him. Bodies, at least half a dozen, lay scattered and face down. The one immediately in front of him seemed to be partly submerged, as if sinking into the ground. Horses lay on their sides; most dead with stiff legs, while those that had survived were wounded and bleeding with the whites of their eyes flashing their distress. Other objects lay scattered in between: a hat, a water canteen, a gunbelt, and an upright lance with feathers that fluttered in the light breeze.

Walt and Ned dismounted, each with his rifle in hand, and quickly moved from body to body, to briefly kneel, look, reach out and touch, before moving on, while William sat in his saddle, frozen.

'Over here,' called Ned. 'This one is still alive.'

Walt ran across to join him, his boot heels kicking sand into the air.

Ned rolled the man over and propped him up slowly, then slid his knee under the head as a support, while Walt called to William to bring over a water canteen.

But William Lundy sat, immobile and shaking slightly. Walt called again, louder this time.

'Water. Bill, bring me a canteen.'

William remained transfixed, as if spellbound.

Walt pulled his pistol from the holster, cocked the hammer and fired a shot into the air.

William jumped in the saddle, breaking the hex.

'Water,' called Walt again.

William slid from the saddle, then fell to the ground, stumbling backwards. He scrambled to his feet, pulled a full canteen from the second packhorse and ran with faltering steps over to Walt.

When he stopped at the man's feet he could see the blood that covered all of the front of his shirt, down to the trouser belt.

'Water,' said Walt with an outstretched hand.

William handed him the canteen, his eyes fixed on the man's chest, which jerked as he tried to drink from the flask being held to his lips. Then he coughed and William saw water mixed with blood run from the corners of his mouth, just as the man's eyes opened and he called to William as if in fright, 'Who are you?'

William was just about to answer when he realized that the man's hair had been peeled back, so that it now bunched up high near the crown and rested on Ned's leg.

'Settlers? Where are the settlers?' asked Walt with urgency.

'Gone.' The word was choked from the bloody mouth.

'Where?'

'They went.' He spoke with stilted

effort. 'We stayed to fight.'

'Taylor? Where is Taylor?'

The wounded man coughed. 'Water.'

'Jason Taylor. Where is Jason Taylor?'

'Gone with the settlers. Water.'

Walt held the canteen steady as the man tried to drink and asked, 'Is Louis Bolan here?'

Water flooded from the man's mouth before he coughed again, then said with difficulty, 'I'm Louis Bolan.'

Walt looked around at the slaughter as Ned placed his hand on the wounded man's shoulder and glanced up at the lance with fluttering feathers.

'Choctaw or Chickasaw?' he asked.

Bolan shook his head a little. 'No. The Mexicans and their renegades did this to make it look like Chickasaw.'

'Mexicans?' said Walt. 'What the hell are Mexicans . . . ' He paused before he asked, thinking it couldn't be so. 'Was this the work of Eloy Cobos?'

With effort Louis Bolan nodded his head.

'So renegades are riding with Cobos

and his Mexicans?'

Bolan nodded his head again slowly as he spoke with visible distress.

'The Mexicans did this to me, not the Indians.'

'Cobos,' murmured Walt in disbelief as he looked at the dry blood matted in the folds of skin and dark hair. He lifted the canteen back to the wounded man's lips and said, 'Another drink, Mr Bolan.'

Louis Bolan tried to take another mouthful but most of the water ran from his mouth.

'When did this happen?' asked Walt.

Bolan coughed up some more water, then gasped out in a slur, 'Yesterday, late.'

Walt looked up over Ned's shoulder and into the distance; deep in thought as he tried to work out how far the wagons would have been able to travel in that time.

Then suddenly Bolan reached up and grabbed Walt's shirt. With glaring eyes he called out, 'Arbuckle.'

'What?' said Walt, confused.

'Have mercy,' said Bolan, his voice now back to a whisper, but with his bloodied fist still gripping tight and pulling Walt towards him. 'Don't leave me like this.'

It was the appeal of a distraught and exhausted man in agony from his fatal wounds. Blood was now running freely from his mouth as he tried desperately to speak and be heard.

Walt leant in close and could see the plea for compassion in Bolan's eyes as the despairing Frenchman whispered, 'Have mercy. Shoot me.'

16

Too Honest

After Midday

There was no sign that the attackers had given chase after the settlers.

Walt asked Ned if he could make any sense of such an isolated attack.

'Feuding, maybe,' he replied.

'Feuding over what?'

'Don't know, but I'll bet there's money in it somewhere.' Ned rubbed his thumb and a forefinger together. 'Always is when men are killed like this.'

'Maybe,' said Walt as he looked around.

'You're after Cobos, aren't you?' asked Ned.

Walt kept looking. 'I have a warrant for him.'

'What's he done?'

'He killed a marshal near Muskogee, amongst other things.'

'Bolan? What were you after him for?'

'Much the same; he killed a marshal over near Tahlequah.'

'And Taylor?'

Walt looked away. 'That's personal.'

'No warrant?'

'No.'

'Is he with the wagons?'

'As far as I can tell.'

'So who are we going after, then? Cobos or Taylor?'

'Taylor,' said Walt without hesitation.

'Personal business first, eh?' said Ned.

'You'll still get paid,' said Walt, his words terse.

'Then after Taylor, it's Cobos?'

'Not out here,' said Walt. 'I need to get him on even ground, and on his own. Not when he's riding around massacring those who might be getting in his way.'

Ned half-grinned. 'You won't catch me complaining. Easier to take on one man than a bunch of loco Mexicans who have taken up scalping.' Then he nudged Walt and glanced over at William Lundy, who was kneeling, leaning back on his heels with the water canteen on his lap. His eyes were wide and although he was looking towards Walt and Ned it was with a stare that passed straight through them.

'Bill,' called Walt, but he got no response. He called again, this time louder. 'Bill.' But still he received no response, so he walked over to the reporter and crouched before him. Yet William seemed not to notice his presence. Walt could see the lips trembling slightly as he reached up and gently tapped the side of the young journalist's face with his open palm.

'Bill, come on, we've got to go, and we need to get our minds back on the job.'

'Never seen a dead man before,' whispered William Lundy. 'Not one that has been shot and scalped. I've written about men being shot, but I have never seen it before today.'

Walt nodded sympathetically. 'No, it's never like you think it might be.'

'I will never forget what I've seen today. The brutality.'

Walt gave another pat to the cheek. 'Bill, don't dwell. It will do you no good. Push these thoughts out of your mind.'

'But how?'

'By busying yourself,' said Walt. 'Never sit idle.'

'I have nothing to busy myself with. I have nothing to do here of any useful purpose. I should go back.' William Lundy dropped his head.

'Do what you are good at,' said Walt. 'Get your notepad out and start reporting.' Then he said without sympathy, 'And stop feeling sorry for yourself.'

William looked up with surprise.

'So you've seen death up close for the first time, and you've seen the violence that men can do, and now you've seen the reality behind what excites your readers back east. What are you going to do, Bill Lundy? Run away and hide?'

The water welled in William's eyes. 'What should I do, then?' he shouted in angry defeat.

'Report on the reality, straight up and true, and thank the good Lord that you're still alive. You never know, today you may have learnt the most important lesson of your life.'

When Walt returned to Ned he caught the look in the old man's blue eyes. He paused before scuffing the ground with his right boot and saying softly, 'Was I too harsh?'

'No,' said Ned. 'Just too honest.'

17

Arbuckle

Sunday 28 August

The settlers had taken off like jackrabbits, or so Ned said as he crouched, inspecting their wagon tracks where they entered the creek.

'But where are they going?' asked Walt.

'Somewhere they don't want anyone to follow,' said Ned.

'This is taking way too long,' said Walt. 'Is the sign there that all the wagons are still together?'

'Best as I can tell. Would be safer if they stuck together. If they separate they can be picked off, one by one,' said Ned.

Walt nodded in agreement.

'They seem to know where they are going,' said Ned.

'Why is that?'

'They just aren't taking the easiest way to put distance between them and where they were. They were going north but now it looks like they are heading east.'

'Maybe they are just looking for somewhere to hide,' said Walt.

Ned shrugged. 'I don't think so.'

That night when they made camp William Lundy conscientiously pulled out his notebook and quietly began to quiz Ned on his life as a buffalo hunter, and before then as a Confederate marksman. Ned was happy to reminisce; however, the life and times of Walter Garfield remained a mystery. When those brief moments allowed for William to sit and talk with Walt, he invariably changed the subject. So, frustrated, the New York correspondent asked him about other matters.

'Ned told me you were carrying papers for the arrest of Mr Bolan because he killed a marshal.'

'That's correct,' said Walt. 'But in

145

what exact circumstances I don't know. Maybe he was provoked.'

William thought this seemed an odd thing to say, so he said: 'Maybe his lawless life finally caught up with him?'

'Maybe,' said Walt, 'but I doubt it. Life doesn't have a habit of working out like that. A preacher may tell you that good triumphs over evil, but I have yet to see it.'

'But if Bolan killed a marshal, then he was evil, wasn't he?'

Walt looked into his tin cup before he sipped, then pulled a face at the bitterness of the coffee.

'Bolan stayed with his men and fought a rearguard action that allowed the settlers to escape. So he wasn't all bad.' Then he added, 'If only people were all good or all bad, wouldn't that make life real easy.'

'But some are, aren't they?'

'If they are, then I've yet to meet one.' Walt's response was laced with a touch of scorn. 'Even the unspoiled eventually spoil.'

William didn't know what he meant and he flicked back through the pages of his notebook.

'Why did the Mexicans make the attack look like it was done by the Indians? Was it just to hide their crime? Or was it to get the blame put on the Indians for another reason?'

Walt shrugged.

'The Indian chiefs would know that they didn't do it, wouldn't they?' questioned William.

'Who's going to believe them?' said Ned. 'Even if all the chiefs swear an oath it wasn't them. Out here, if one is guilty then they are all seen to be guilty.'

'Could it start a war against the tribes?'

'There already is one,' said Walt. 'Soon the only Indian we'll get to see will be on a coin.'

'You sound like a Quaker,' said William.

'No, not me. Some people in this world deserve to die for their deeds.

Just I've never seen the reason for it to be the Indians.'

'But they have killed settlers in cold blood.'

'And we kill them in return.'

'Isn't that justice?'

'No, it's just payback. It's not even retribution cos we'll kill ten for every settler killed.'

William turned his pad towards the light of the fire as he wrote, then paused and asked Walt, 'What does Arbuckle mean?'

'You mean Arbuckle's coffee?' said Walt, looking down into his coffee mug.

'No, I don't think so. It's what Louis Bolan said. Arbuckle.'

'Is that what he said? I just thought he was speaking French.'

William continued to study his notepad before calling to Ned: 'Does Arbuckle mean anything to you?'

Ned sat there shaking his head. 'Arbuckle. The only Arbuckle I know out here is Fort Arbuckle to the east. But that was abandoned a little while back. There's no one there any more. Just the buildings.'

Walt sat upright. 'A fort! Structures that can be defended. Where's my saddle valise, my maps?' He was looking around with concern, as if he had just been robbed.

'Here,' said William. 'I've been leaning against it.'

Walt snatched up the valise and rummaged through the contents until he found his maps.

'Ned, show me where this fort is, on the map.'

18

The Newlyweds

Monday 29 August — Mid Morning
The shot cracked through the air to surprise those who heard it, like lightning out of a clear blue sky. In an instant the bullet struck the tree branch just above Walt's head with a thump. Ned, who was just behind Walt, yelled out, 'Yeeee,' and pulled his horse and the two packhorses back down into the creek to where William Lundy was getting ready to take his mount up the embankment.

Walt turned in the saddle and half-slid then fell to the ground as he sought safety behind the trunk of the large saw-tooth oak.

'Hold your fire,' he yelled. 'We're friendly.'

The response from the nearest

building of the old fort from where the first shot had been fired was a second shot.

'I need a flag to wave,' yelled Walt towards the creek line. 'Bill, you got anything white on you?'

'Don't think so,' came the call from back below the creek bank.

'Then get my washbag. With my bedroll on one of the horses. My calico washbag.'

William dismounted, splashed over to the first packhorse and frantically pulled open the flap on a canvas pocket. He tried a second, then a third pocket before he found the bag. He ran up to the bank of the creek and called to Walt.

'I've got it. But it's more grey than white. I could give it a wash, in the creek. Might make it more — '

'Just throw it here. I just need something to wave that's kinda white. And I need it now.'

William swung the bag of toiletries above his head, then let it go. It landed in the open, some five or six paces out from the tree that Walt was now hiding behind.

'Geezes, who taught you to throw?' called Walt. He sucked in a deep breath, then said, 'One, two, three,' quickly, and rushed out and grabbed the bag. As he turned back to the safety of the tree a third shot cracked through the air. Walt scrambled, like a rabbit trying to find a hole. Once protected by the tree again, he emptied the contents of the washbag at his feet, then looked about for a stick. He saw one just behind the tree, and swiftly he tied the calico bag to the small dried branch. He poked out his improvised flag and began waving as he yelled, 'Hold your fire. Hold your fire. We are friendly.'

There was no response but he kept waving.

At last a voice called from the building directly in front of him.

'How many are you?'

'Three, with five horses.'

'Who are you?'

Walt went to say his name but stopped and called back: 'A deputy US marshal.'

'Where are you from?'

'Marshal's office at Fort Worth and assigned to the Indian Territory.'

Some muffled whoops and hollers were heard coming from the building before a call came back.

'Come on over, Marshal.'

Walt stepped out slowly and called back towards the creek. 'Follow after me, Ned, so that they may see who we are.'

'I'm coming,' called Ned.

Walt was almost up to the white-washed picket fence that ran across the front of the long building when a door opened and a man stepped out on to the veranda.

'No disrespect meant; we just thought you might be Indians. My name's Wesley Hefan and it was my wife Elisa who was on watch. She just saw someone come out of the creek and thought — '

Walt interrupted to introduce himself.

'Garfield. Walt Garfield.' He looked around at the other buildings that made up the old fort. 'Are you the people who were travelling with Louis Bolan?'

Hefan smiled with relief. 'Yes, we've been expecting him, and then when he didn't come, well, we've all become a little jumpy. Is he with you?'

'No, there are just the three of us.'

'Have you seen him?'

'Yes. Yes I have,' said Walt slowly.

'Have you spoken to him?'

'Yes.'

'Where is he?'

Walt looked around before he answered: 'Where you left him.'

'When is he coming? One of his men is here with us and brought us to this place, but Bolan is in charge.'

'He won't be coming,' said Walt.

The settler looked confused. He asked: 'Will any of them be coming?'

Walt shook his head, then said

quietly, 'No, they won't. They're all dead.'

The colour in Wes Hefan's face drained and he seemed to shake on the spot before he spoke again. 'All of them? Dead?'

'Yes,' said Walt. 'But we spoke to Louis before he passed away and he gave word of where you had gone.'

The settler didn't respond.

'How many are here?' asked Walt.

Hefan still didn't speak, so Walt prompted him again.

At last Hefan said, 'Seven families, five wagons. Thirty-four in all. And Pat Wheeler, our guide.'

'Going where?'

'Most to take up land with other settlers around Smith Paul's Valley. One family wants to go further west to Wolf Creek, and one is going all the way to Santa Fe and on to California.'

'And who would that be?' asked Walt.

'Mr Taylor and his wife.'

'His wife?' The air seemed to be sucked out of Walt's lungs and he buckled a little. 'Did you say his wife?'

'Yes, Marie.'

'Marie or Maria?'

'Marie.'

'Geeze!' said Walt through clenched teeth.

'You know them?'

'Yeah, I know them all right.'

'They'll be pleased to see you, then.'

'That,' said Walt, 'I doubt very much. Where are they now?'

'The Taylors?'

'Yes, the newlywed Taylors.'

'They are over on the other side of the compound, guarding the eastern approaches. I can go and get them if you like.'

'No, don't do that. Let me surprise them both. I've been kind of looking forward to catching up unannounced.'

19

Peas in a Pod

Ten Minutes Later
Jason Taylor lay flat on his back, out cold. Walt stood over the body, clenching then shaking his hand.

'Geezes,' he said and sucked the air in through his teeth. 'You always did have a hard head.'

'That's what he always said about you.' The words were spat out fast and furious in a Mexican accent from the attractive woman with fire in her eyes. She leant over Taylor, her hand pressed upon his forehead. 'Does that make you happy, that you have hit him?'

'Not enough,' said Walt, opening and closing his fingers to relieve the pain from the blow to the side of Taylor's head.

'Do you want to hit me? A woman?'

'Don't tempt me.'

The woman bit at her lip. 'I know you are hurt in your heart, but it was not what I wanted. It was not my plan.'

'You had a plan?' Walt flexed his fingers again. 'Yeah, I bet you did, because it sure took me by surprise.'

'No,' she said. 'Not a plan like that. It just happened, we fell in love.'

'Oh,' said Walt, 'that's all right, then. It was love. Seems I've heard that before.'

'You are hurt.'

'Whatever gave you that idea?'

Jason Taylor raised a shoulder, then slowly sat up to rest his arms on his knees.

'I saw that coming,' he said with a slight slur as he moved his jaw from side to side.

'Then you should have ducked,' said Walt.

'No, you needed to get it out of your system.'

'You think one punch is going to do

that? I've chased you halfway across Mexico, through Louisiana, across Texas and into Indian Territory, and you think I came all this way just to sock you in the jaw?'

'Will you leave us, Marie. I need to talk to Walt. He's a little upset.'

'He will kill you.'

'No he won't.'

'Don't bet on it,' said Walt.

'Mr Hefan,' said Jason Taylor, 'would you take Marie away so that I may speak with Walt?'

'Marie? What happened to Maria?' asked Walt.

Taylor didn't respond to Walt's question and waited as Wesley Hefan escorted the woman from the room. He then said, 'What did you come for, Walt? Me? Marie?'

'Why don't we start with the gold leases first, then we'll get to you and Maria.'

'The gold leases are long gone.'

'Long gone? Gone where?'

'They've just gone.'

'What, up in smoke?'

'No, sold. We used them to finance our . . . ' Taylor moved his jaw again.

'Escape?' said Walt.

'Our trip to California. Anyway the leases were as much mine and Marie's as yours. We worked them too.'

'Is that a fact? Then where is my share?'

'It's all gone. It paid for the wagon, the livestock, the provisions, and the protection through the Indian Territory. There is no more left.'

'How much did you get?'

'Three thousand dollars. A thousand dollars for each.'

'Is that all? The mines will generate a hundred times that.'

'No they won't. I was lucky to get what I got. You've just talked yourself into believing that. Just like you talked yourself into every other half-baked scheme in your life.'

'What?'

'Let's face it, Walt, you're a dreamer and you're a . . . '

'What?'

'No, it doesn't matter.'

'No, go on, say it. Get it off your chest.'

'OK then, you're a drunk. And a womanizer too.'

'Drunk and womanizer? Well, ain't that rich, coming from the man who likes to pull a cork or two himself, and has just run off with my wife.'

'She was sick of your drinking.'

'I only drink if it's around. If it's not then I'm fine.'

'Yeah, but you can sniff out the dregs of a whiskey bottle lying under a cactus bush.'

'You should hear yourself, Champagne Charlie Taylor.'

'Those days are well behind me. I just want to settle down, with my wife.'

The look on Walt's face was one of amazement. 'Are you forgetting something? She's married to me. Remember?'

'Not any more. That was under Mexican law. We are in the United States now.'

'Since when did crossing the border change the state of marriage? And what about the church? We were married in the church. Maria's church. Her uncle was the priest. Or have you both forgotten?'

'No, but we met with the Archbishop of New Orleans and explained the situation, and he has annulled her past marriage.'

'On what grounds?'

'Your bigamous ways.'

'What bigamous ways?' Walt was starting to pace back and forwards.

'During the war.'

'I didn't marry anyone during the war.'

Taylor moved his jaw with his hand. 'I was sure that you had, but maybe I was mistaken. Anyway, what's done is done.'

'You made it up, didn't you? You told Maria that I had been married before. Geezes!, Well, haven't you stitched me up nicely? Stole my El Oro gold leases that I pegged and registered myself; run off with my wife; got her unmarried so that she could marry you, then sold a potential fortune for a few thousand dollars so that you could have a new lovey-dovey life in sunny California.'

'I expected that you would be a little upset, at first. But you will see it different in time.'

Walt shook his head in disbelief. 'And how do you figure that?'

'I'm older. I understand what time can do. And besides, time is running out for me. This is my last shot at happiness, and maybe for Marie too.'

'Is that the same happiness that you gave my mother?'

'I was younger then.'

'Well, isn't that a good excuse?'

'Truth is I was once exactly like you, Walter, but I am now a new man. I have changed.'

'New man! What hogwash. You haven't changed. You were a rat, you're still a rat, and you'll always be a rat.'

'Walter, my son, we are peas in the same pod, but I have done something about it. I have turned over a new leaf.'

'Don't you start that 'Walter my son' bull. Peas in a pod! A new leaf! I should have known when I went back to New Orleans after the war and told you about El Oro that you'd eventually spoil it all, just like you did before. And to think my mother, God rest her soul, still had nothing but a kind word for you, right up to the time of her death. She filled my head full of excuses for why you ran out on us, chasing riches. You know, she always said that you would come back. But you had no intention of coming back, did you?'

Taylor said nothing.

'Peas in the same pod?' scoffed Walt. 'If I had a son, I'm damned if I would run out on him and his mother, to leave them to near starve to death.'

'I'm not proud of my past, but what is done is done and there is no going back.'

Walt put his hand on his head and rubbed it in small circles. 'Geezes,' he said.

'Have you come to take Marie back?' asked Taylor.

'Back where?'

'With you.'

Walt patted the crown of his head and let out a long breath.

'Well, up to now that *was* my plan, along with pistol-whipping you and getting back my gold leases. But what use is that now? It's gone, all gone and she wouldn't stay, anyway. I saw how she looked at me with fire, then had doe eyes for you. I'm not that blind.'

'You expected it would be different, didn't you?'

Walt didn't answer.

'It always is with kin. Sort of complicated. I don't have any money to pay you back for the leases. But maybe . . . over time.' It was said as a conciliatory declaration.

'You must have some left. You can't have spent all of three thousand on a wagon, stock and supplies?'

Taylor gave a small cough, then said

quietly, 'I had to make a donation to the church.'

'Why?'

'The archbishop said it would help with the annulment.'

Walt nodded his head slowly. 'I bet it did.'

'In time though, if I saved, I could — '

Walt cut his father short. 'Don't go making promises you can't keep.'

'OK,' said Jason Taylor, brushing off Walt's response with visible relief. 'What now? Are we free to go when Bolan returns?'

'Bolan isn't returning. He's dead, along with those who were with him.'

'Did the Indians kill them all? Why? I spoke to him just before we left and he said that he knew who had been shadowing us and that he would talk to them. It was just a precaution that we came here.' Jason Taylor stood up, still rubbing his chin. 'Are we now at risk from an Indian attack?'

'It's not the Indians you should be worried about.'

'Who, then?'

'The Mexicans.'

'What Mexicans?'

Walt looked towards the door. 'One of Bolan's men is here. I need to speak to him and find out what he knows.'

'To find out what we may be up against?'

'I know what we are up against,' said Walt. 'I've seen it. I want to know what this is all about, and to see if it's likely that they'll come here.'

'What would any Mexicans want with peaceful settlers?'

'You're not classing yourself as a peaceful settler now, are you?'

'That's precisely what I am.'

'Well, excuse me for thinking all this time that you were a thieving, cheating, wife-stealing rat.'

'I said, I have changed my ways.' Taylor leaned in a little to study Walt's badge on his chest. 'And I see that you are now with the law.'

'That's right,' said Walt.

'Seems we have both adopted new lives.'

'Mine was out of necessity,' said Walt. 'It was the only way I could get the horses and provisions to chase you into Indian Territory and all the way to California, if I had to.'

'How enterprising — and determined, too, but you always were. However, the settlers here will still think that you are here to help and protect them.'

'Yeah, I'm learning how this badge thing works.'

'You could always take the badge off and ride away.'

'I could, but I won't.'

'No, I'm sure you won't. You always did have a sense of honour in an odd sort of way. I think you must have got it from me.'

'Oh, knock it off. If I got it from anywhere it would have been from my mother, not you.'

'Ah, she was a fine woman,' said Jason Taylor, casting his eyes to the ceiling.

'So was Maria until you got into her ear.'

'Still is.'

'Yeah, but she has a rotten taste in men.'

'That's true too,' conceded Jason Taylor. Then, looking down at the floor, he added, 'Twice.'

20

Cobos

An Hour Later

'So you're Bolan's man who guided the settlers here?'

'I ride with Bolan, but I have ridden with others like him,' said Pat Wheeler with a look of defiance.

Walt noted the attitude and thought it better to get this over and done with, quick.

'The men you were riding with, this time, are all dead, and that includes Louis Bolan.'

Wheeler didn't blink but he had been caught off balance, so Walt played his ace and said, 'He was scalped but still alive, just, when we got to him. He managed to speak and lead the three of us here to you.'

Wheeler glanced quickly at Ned and

William, who were standing to one side of Walt with Jason Taylor. Then he said slowly, 'All dead? Are you sure?'

'That's about the only thing I am sure of,' said Walt. 'The attack looked like it was Indian, but Bolan said it wasn't. Do you know who it could have been?'

Walt could see Wheeler weighing up exactly what he should say. Finally, he said, 'We'd seen some Indians, just a few, but they were keeping back and just looking. They do it all the time, so none of us was too concerned, except for Lou; he was a little on edge. He'd been that way since we left Henrietta in a hurry, after he'd found out that the marshal who shot Frank Allen in Atoka was in town and asking after him.' He looked at Walt's star. 'Which I guess is you?'

Walt nodded. 'And just how did he find that out?'

'Lou had got the word of Frank's killing by telegram. Frank owed Lou money from some business they had done in Atoka. The clerk in the Atoka telegraph office is a cousin of Jim Cole, he rides . . . ' Wheeler stopped and corrected himself, slowly. 'He rode with us.' Wheeler's head hung a little as he fell silent.

'Go on,' said Walt.

'Then Big John told Lou that a new arrival from Atoka was asking after him and that he was a marshal who had fixed a squabble out the front of his saloon.' Then Wheeler licked his bottom lip. 'So Lou told the settlers that we had to go, and we left, real sharp. Then when we saw the Indian scouts following us he told me to take the settlers to the old fort and that he would follow.'

'Why?'

'The Indians were young renegades, and a little unpredictable. But they were working for the Mexicans.'

'What Mexicans?'

Wheeler shrugged. 'There is this band of Mexicans who rode in from Texas about two months ago. Lou did some business with them but it went bad.'

'And the name of the head Mexican?'

'Cobos. Eloy Cobos.'

'OK, you're being straight with me, because that's the name Louis Bolan gave me. So don't hold back, because I need to know if Cobos is coming after you.'

Pat Wheeler's eyes flashed but he remained silent.

'Does Cobos know you? Does he know that you were riding with Bolan?'

Wheeler nodded his head as if in fright.

'So, if Cobos killed Louis Bolan and all who rode with him, is he also after you?'

Wheeler quickly licked a dry bottom lip. 'Lou had said that he was going to talk to Cobos and work it all out.'

'Work out what, exactly?'

'The trading with the Indians and what had gone wrong.'

'Trading what?'

'Trading guns and ammunition with the Indians.'

'And what went wrong?'

'It was working fine but Cobos wanted more and he thought he could get it when he started dealing with a buck called Taku who was leading the renegades.'

Wheeler was now speaking fast. 'Lou said the Mexicans had come up with this idea to squeeze in on the railroads by staging Indian raids against the surveyors and the workers when they started to lay track south. Cobos then planned to sell protection to the railroads, call off the renegades, and keep the profit.' Wheeler drew in a quick breath. 'He said Cobos was also going to use Taku to raid the cattle drives coming through the Territory from the south before they got to the railheads, then get the railroads to pay for protection of the cattlemen as well.'

'What was Bolan's response?'

'Lou saw an opportunity. He went

up to Kansas and told the railroads about Cobos and his plans, and they rewarded him by working out a deal for Lou to protect the settlers. The railroad company wants to establish townships down the line using the government land grants they had been given, so they need the settlers to keep coming.'

'Go on,' Walt said, for Wheeler was now clearly agitated.

'When Cobos heard about what Lou had done he got real riled. Lou set up a meeting to smooth things over and said that he would cut the Mexicans in on the deal as there were plenty of settlers to protect.'

'Were you at that meeting?'

Wheeler nodded. 'Cobos seemed OK with that and said that he had some new plans as well. He wanted to set up some travelling whorehouses, running squaws and opium to the Chinese working on the railroads, but Lou said it was a dumb idea. The Chinks only get thirty-two a month. 'You have to go for the Anglos,' he said, 'they get twenty more and you have to provide them with white women and hard liquor because that's what they pay big for, not squaws and peace pipes. He also said that there was more money to be made out of cattlemen than railroad labourers.'

'What did Cobos say?'

'He got real upset being called dumb to his face in front of everybody.'

'Then what?' said Walt.

'We left. I was a bit worried, knowing what Cobos is like, but Lou didn't seem to care.' Wheeler rubbed the palm of his right hand down the side of his trouser leg, then quickly licked his dry lips again and continued:

'A few days later, when we were cutting a deal with some Indians on a load of old army Henrys, I saw a young buck in the mob called Nika. I pointed him out to Lou and told him that Nika rode for Cobos. Lou called him over and Nika couldn't keep his eyes off the Yellowboy that Lou had in his hand. It was brand new and as shiny as hell. It seemed to mesmerize Nika, so Lou let him hold it, then fire it. He was a good shot too. A steady hand and could hit a dime at a hundred paces. So Lou said to Nika that he could have the rifle as a gift. The Indian's eyes were like moons when he heard that. He couldn't believe it. Then Lou said, only if he killed Cobos with the rifle.'

Walt could hear the movement behind him. It was William. He turned slightly and saw the reporter standing with his notepad in his hand and his mouth slightly open.

'Did Nika agree?'

'Oh yeah, he agreed in a flash, so Lou gave him the rifle and a marked .44 cartridge to do the job. He told Nika he wanted the marked cartridge case back after the shot had been fired. And he wanted it back personally from Nika, to show that he had kept his side of the bargain.'

'So what happened?'

'Nika rode straight back to Cobos

and told him about the deal, because Lou got a small package in Henrietta. It was the marked bullet he'd given Nika and it was wrapped in a note from Cobos, saying he could have it back, because he had one just like it for Lou, and that he was going to deliver it personally, out of the barrel of a gun.'

'How did Bolan take the threat?'

'Lou is a hard man and it didn't seem to worry him too much, at first. He said he would talk again with Cobos and smooth it out.'

'What did you think?'

'Lou can handle himself; he's been up against worse. But then, when I recognized that one of the Indians following us after we left Henrietta was Nika, I knew something was up.'

'You told Bolan?'

'Straight away, and that's when he told me to take the settlers here and he would follow.'

'Well, maybe you are in the clear,' said Walt. 'Maybe this whole thing was just between Bolan and Cobos?'

Wheeler shuffled his feet. 'No, there's more to it than that.'

'What exactly?'

Pat Wheeler licked his lips, then rubbed the back of his hand across his mouth.

'It was my idea that we should get Nika to kill Cobos. I knew Nika, because I once rode with the Mexicans. I sold the idea to Lou and I also explained to Nika what he had to do.'

Walt shook his head. 'You once rode for Cobos, too?'

'Just for a while.'

'So how many ride with Cobos now?'

'Four other Mexicans; one is his brother, the other three are his cousins, and usually about four or five Americans.'

'And renegades with Taku?'

'About a hundred.'

Jason Taylor, who was standing next to Ned, let out a slow, low whistle. 'A hundred!'

'If Cobos turns up here, is he likely

to bring Taku and his bucks with him?' asked Walt.

'Yes,' said Wheeler in a clear voice.

William Lundy let out a little gasp and dropped his notepad and pencil to clatter upon the floor.

21

Parts of the Puzzle

A Little Later

Pat Wheeler licked his dry lips. 'I need to get a drink of water.'

Walt nodded, scratching his chin in thought.

As Wheeler left the room William Lundy asked, 'What do we do now?'

'Simple,' said Jason Taylor as he watched the door close. 'If this Mexican, Cobos, turns up then we hand over Wheeler and go on our way.'

Walt threw a glare at his father.

Jason Taylor looked over to see his son, Ned and William staring at him in cold silence.

'I was only joking. Lighten up a little, boys,' he said and smiled, his face radiating charm. William relaxed and walked towards Taylor.

'I'm William Lundy,' he said, extending his hand in introduction.

'Jason Taylor,' came the reply.

'Oh,' said William. 'The man that the marshal is after?'

'Yes, that's me. Walt's been wanting to catch up with his father for some time.'

There was silence from William and Ned as they both turned to look at Walt.

'It's sort of a family reunion before I continue on my way,' said Jason Taylor.

'Where to?' asked William.

'California.'

'How exciting, but such a long journey,' said William.

'True, but I've done it before, in '49 with Walt and his mother. He was a toddler then. Bright, mind you. He was just five. My, my, how he has grown.'

William looked across at Walt. 'I can see the likeness,' he said.

Jason Taylor smiled. 'Yes I know, just like two peas in a pod.'

'You must be very proud of your son,

now that he's a deputy US marshal,' said William.

Taylor rocked on his heels. 'As a peacock.'

'You are a peacock,' said Walt without any hint of humour.

'Is your wife with you?' asked William.

'Yes, she is,' said Taylor.

'Walt's mother?'

Taylor cast his eyes to the floor. 'No. Alas, she has passed on. I have just remarried.'

'Oh, that would now be the marshal's stepmother?'

Jason Taylor pulled his head up quickly.

'Why, yes it would.'

'I would like to meet her and ask about the rigours of the trail for a woman,' said William Lundy. 'I'm a reporter from the *New York Times* on assignment with the marshal as he dispenses law and order in the Indian Territory.'

Jason Taylor stopped his rocking.

'Oh, a reporter?'

'That's right.'

'From New York?'

'Yes.'

Taylor shook his head slowly. 'She's tired and busy right now. Maybe you can speak to her later.'

'I wouldn't bother if I was you, Bill,' said Walt. 'I've tried talking to her, and I couldn't get any sense out of her whatsoever.'

'Maybe you weren't listening,' said Jason Taylor. 'In fact, I don't think you've been listening to Marie in years.'

'And I suppose you have?'

'Yes, I have. Women like to speak and be listened to.'

Walt was getting annoyed.

Jason Taylor lifted his hands into the air with his fingers splayed.

'Anyway, enough of such small talk. What I want to know is what my son, the marshal, is going to do to resolve this unfortunate situation.'

Walt kept his gaze on his father. 'I don't know yet. But if I thought for a minute that staking you out in that courtyard as a sacrificial offering to Cobos and his renegades would do any good, then I'd be whittling the stakes right now.' Walt pulled off his hat, hit it against the side of his leg and strode out of the room.

'He's a little upset with me at the moment,' said Taylor.

'What over?' asked William.

'Oh, we had a joint venture going on down in Mexico and it sort of went belly-up. Nobody's fault, just one of those things. But Walt was kind of betting it would all turn out all right and that his boat would come in.'

'But it didn't?'

'No, I doubt if it even set sail. All a young man's folly, really. I tried to tell him, but sometimes children just won't listen to a parent. Don't pass that on, he can be a bit tetchy about the subject.'

'So you all left Mexico and came back to the United States?'

'We did, but not together. My wife

and I decided it would be better to just leave, without the formality of farewells. They can sometimes be so . . . ' he paused, then said, 'emotional.'

'But it has been to the advantage of the citizens of our nation, hasn't it? Now that your son has followed and joined the marshals.'

Jason Taylor gave the proposition some thought, then said slowly, 'Yes, I suppose in a way it has.'

'Mr Taylor, could I interview you later, on the marshal's past? It would help me to understand him better. He is somewhat reluctant to say too much to me.'

'I'm not surprised.'

'He is a very humble man,' said William.

'Humble?' questioned Taylor with a quiet smile. 'Yes, I'd be delighted to fill in any missing parts of the puzzle that is my son, Walter Douglas Garfield.'

22

Stampeding Buffalo

Evening

In fading light, Walt walked around the abandoned fort with Wesley Hefan so that he could get a feel for the layout. Wes confirmed that all of the buildings were bare of anything that hadn't been nailed down.

'Even took the bell out of the bellhouse,' he said. 'But the structures are all weather-tight and there is fresh water in the well.'

The now empty buildings were formed around a central courtyard with its tall flagpole, where a company of cavalry had once assembled. On the east side were the stables, smithy and livery store. To the west were the officers' quarters and the commander's cottage. To the north were the soldiers' barracks with its small bellhouse perched upon its roof to call the men to parade.

To the south was the largest of the buildings, which housed the soldiers' mess hall with its separate outdoor kitchen, a guardroom with a small cell, and four separate rooms for headquarters staff. It was in this building, with its long veranda down one side, that most of the settlers were camped.

'I think you should move everyone into the mess hall building,' said Walt.

'I thought it would be better to have some sentry posts in the other buildings,' said Wes. 'I was using my army training. I served in the Georgia First Regiment under Wallace.'

'If the Georgia Firsts were here I'd do the same, but isolated outposts without supporting fire will just be picked off.'

Wes nodded slowly in agreement while his face showed his concern.

'I know it has its risks,' said Walt, 'but at least we can control everyone under the same roof and defend all sides of this building.'

'You know the last of the troops that were here have only just left,' said Wes. 'Around March, I'd say; you can see where their names and dates have been carved on the wall of the mess hall.'

Walt glanced around. 'Yeah, that would be about right. I seem to have spent a lifetime being at the wrong place at the wrong time and usually by only a whisker or two.'

'Makes it worse somehow, doesn't it?' said Wes. 'This could have been our haven, but now it's just our — '

Walt quickly changed the subject of possible pending doom.

'Wes, I'm going to get Bill and Ned to make out an inventory of the arms, ammunition and provisions that we have, then I want to address all the men.'

'And the women?'

'No, not at the moment. I don't want to alarm them any more than we have to.'

An hour later Walt addressed the men standing before him.

'The situation is this,' he said firmly. 'We have seven families consisting of you eight men, ten women and sixteen children. A total of thirty-four, plus Wheeler,' Walt nodded towards Pat Wheeler, 'and the three of us. A grand total of thirty-eight.'

He pushed his hat back a little and turned to William Lundy. 'Could you read the count on weapons and ammunition, Bill?'

William stepped forward with his notepad in his hand.

'I can advise of,' he looked down to read, 'seven rifles, three shotguns, and two handguns. Plus Mr Wheeler, Ned and the marshal each have a rifle and a handgun. I also have one handgun. This gives us an arsenal of nineteen weapons. And our stock of ammunition is approximately two thousand cartridges or balls and caps.'

William was about to close his notepad when he added, 'And we also have five wagons, twelve oxen, eight mules, and six horses, along with sundry provisions.'

'OK,' said Walt, pushing his hat back a little further. 'In theory we can arm nineteen men and women, and use those who aren't armed to act as observers and distribute the ammunition.' Walt scratched his forehead. 'And we need to be real careful that we match the right ammunition to the right weapons. Especially when the shooting starts.'

Some of the men started to look nervous before one said, 'What are we up against, Marshal?'

'I was coming to that. In truth I don't know, but it's best that we plan for the worst.'

'And what would that be?' asked Wesley Hefan.

Walt took off his hat and patted the crown of his head a couple of times.

'It could be more than one hundred.'

The gasp from the men was audible.

'More than a hundred Indians?' one settler said in astonishment.

Walt shrugged. 'A mix of Indian renegades, Mexicans and some Americans.'

'Most of us fear the Indians and that's why we paid for protection. But Mexicans? What have the Mexicans got against us?' asked Hefan in bewilderment.

Walt went to speak, but before he could, Jason Taylor said, 'They are outlaws, and they wish to control the peaceful Indian tribes and the land on which you hope to settle, so that they may make themselves rich and powerful. They plan to milk the railroads and the cattlemen of their wealth by fraud and deception and we, unfortunately, have landed in the middle of it.'

The settlers all looked towards Taylor as one of them spoke.

'I thought it was Indians that killed Louis and his men. I want nothing to do with any Mexican bandits. I'm a farmer. If Mexicans and renegades want to attack the railmen and the cattlemen, then that's their business. I say we just leave, and leave now before they find us. This is not our fight. I just want to live in peace.'

'Me too,' said Ned in a voice that was unusually stern. 'I wanted peace before the war. I wanted it during the war, and I wanted it after. But if your neighbour doesn't want peace then you won't get it, not if you get in his way.' Ned had their attention as he spoke.

'And at the moment we are in the way, just as if we were standing before a herd of stampeding buffalo with nowhere to run. So now we have to do what we have to do to survive.'

'And what's that?' said the settler who had declared that they should leave.

'You shoot down the first beast that is just about to run you down so that you can seek shelter behind his carcass. And to do that, it requires that you hold your nerve.'

'Have you done that?' asked another settler.

'I have,' said Ned, his blue eyes now steely cold, 'and I'm still here. If I had tried to run, then I'd be dead. You leave here and you will be chased down and killed, real easy. And that goes for your family too.'

23

No Knight in Shining Armour

Late Evening

Walt was deep in thought. Then he asked, 'Who was that settler, the one Ned answered?'

'About if he had ever shot down a buffalo in a stampede?' asked Jason Taylor.

'No, the other one who wanted no part of this.'

'That was Adam Reed. Why?'

'Maybe he's right,' said Walt. 'Maybe it isn't his fight or that of any of the other settlers.'

'I'd agree with that,' said Jason Taylor. 'But that won't be how Cobos sees it if he comes calling. Ned is right. If your neighbour doesn't want peace and you get in his way, then he'll war with you.'

Walt was looking at the floor, as he

slowly scuffed his boot back and forth.

Taylor continued: 'You and I have dealt with people like Cobos before and we both know that if you show the slightest weakness they will run you down like Ned's stampeding buffaloes.'

'But we are weak,' said Walt. 'Or haven't you noticed?'

'Our numbers are a little on the light side, I'll grant you that, and weapon proficiency is unknown, but hell, when have you or I ever been dealt a full hand? And we always manage to come through. Don't we?'

'I saw what Cobos did to Louis Bolan and his men. It was a slaughter, straight up.'

'So it's a war,' said Taylor, 'and he has an army.'

'But we don't. We don't even have a skirmish line.' The look on Walt's face was grim. 'And we have children here.'

'What are the alternatives?' asked Jason Taylor.

'Maybe we send all the youngsters off with Reed in one wagon?'

'No,' said Marie, who had come into the room to stand close to Taylor. 'If you do that the women will be desperate with worry.'

'Do you want children to be involved in a battle?' asked Walt.

'It is better that they are with their mothers, no matter what, and you should know that, Walter. Besides, Cobos may never come. Have you thought of that? He may not want us. He may not even find us.'

'No, I haven't thought of that,' said Walt.

'Why not?'

'Because he will.' Walt didn't look up. 'There is unfinished business here. It started as a vendetta but now it's a necessity. He killed all of Bolan's men because they were his rivals and they knew of his plans, and that includes Wheeler. By default we now also know of his intentions. Cobos is about to become the kingpin but he needs to cover his tracks. He can't afford for word to get out if his plans are to work.

His security lies in removing all witnesses.'

'And it could also be a contrivance,' said Ned. 'Cobos and the renegades can blame our deaths on the tribes who want peace, and the cavalry will be happy to take revenge. That will then leave Cobos and the renegades with a free run of the Territory.'

'So we stay and fight? Or run?' said Taylor.

'At least we can defend ourselves here. If we leave, we'll be run down in the open and picked off,' said Ned.

'But defend for how long?' said Marie. 'To the death?'

Walt seemed not to be listening, as he kept his head down and mumbled, 'There has to be a way.'

'I'm going to check the watch,' said Taylor. 'But when you figure a way out of this, let me know.'

Walt didn't respond.

'I'll come too,' said William Lundy. He followed Taylor out through the door.

Walt looked up and saw that Marie hadn't moved.

'You still here?'

'Yes.'

'You know he just left?'

'I know,' she said quietly. 'I want to talk, about us.'

Ned looked at the Mexican beauty and saw how she was looking at Walt.

'Time for me to go too.'

'I wouldn't bother, Ned,' said Walt. 'I don't plan on saying much.'

'But I do,' said Marie.

'I'm off,' said Ned. He left the room and closed the door.

Marie clenched her hands and put them to her chin.

'Believe me Walter, I never wanted to hurt you.'

'But?'

Marie creased her brow. 'But what?'

' 'I never wanted to hurt you, Walter, but I did. I smooched up to your father and gave him the opportunity to lift my skirt.' '

Marie's eyes widened and she dropped

her hands to briefly touch her stomach before letting them fall to the sides of her dress.

'You're angry.'

'I thought I was over being angry until we started this conversation, but it's all coming back, and yeah, I'm as angry as hell.'

Tears started to well in Marie's eyes.

'I always wanted you.'

' 'But, I stopped,' ' mimicked Walt.

'No,' said Marie her eyes flashing. '*You* stopped. You stopped noticing me, you stopped talking to me, and you stopped — ' She cut her words short.

'So it's all my fault now?'

'No, but you are no knight in shining armour, either.' The words came out fast and hard.

'I never said I was.'

'But to me you were, once. And then you spent all your time down that mineshaft and did nothing but eat and sleep when you were in our cabin.'

'I was exhausted, for God's sake!'

'Don't swear, Walter, it is not nice.'

'Geezes,' said Walt in clear frustration. 'And what's with this changing your name from Maria to Marie?'

'Jason said that it is best to start anew with a new name.'

'I thought you had already done that by going from Mrs Garfield to Mrs Taylor.'

'I like Marie, it is more American. And I have come here to be American.'

'Oh, so this is what it's really about. You wanted to come and live in America. Then why didn't you just say so?' Walt's voice was raised.

Marie raised her voice back to Walt.

'You would not leave Mexico. You loved it there with your stinking gold mines, and your stinking goldminer friends, and your stinking drinking.' She paused, then said softly, 'And then when it happened — '

Walt was tapping his foot on the floor in quick beats. He cut in: 'I don't suppose that it ever occurred to you that I was doing it for us?'

'Well, you shouldn't have been doing

it for us, just for yourself, because it wasn't what I wanted, but you never asked. Oh no. You may have told the other miners that this was for Maria, but you never asked me what I wanted.'

Walt was getting agitated. 'And what was the other thing, apart from my drinking, that happened?'

Marie looked down at the floor, took in a deep breath and briefly touched her stomach again.

'I want to tell you, so that you know it from me . . . '

But before she could continue there was a soft knock upon the door and it opened to show Ned's face peeking around the corner.

'Yes?' said Walt abruptly.

'Better come and take a look, I think we might have company.'

24

Young Eyes

At the Same Time

When William Lundy accompanied
Jason Taylor to check on those standing
watch, he took the time to ask about
Walt.

'Why is your name Taylor and your
son's is Garfield?' he asked.

Jason Taylor explained that Garfield
was Walt's mother's name. 'I left them
in San Francisco when I went up to the
Trinity River in '50. She was Mrs
Taylor then.'

'And?' asked William, taking his
notepad from the leather satchel that
hung from his shoulder.

'And, I never came back, so she
started over again and changed her
name back,' said Taylor. 'I'm not proud
of it. I ran out on her and Walt. I'd

made some money after nearly five years on the goldfields and I jumped a ship out of San Francisco and sailed around the world on my way back to New Orleans. That was '55, '56.'

William was surprised by this frank admission. 'But why New Orleans?'

'It is where I hail from, and it's where Walter was born, and his mother too. I had spent so much time away from her, prospecting, that I just took for granted that she would have taken up with someone else, or at least that's what I told myself.' Taylor then looked straight at William and said, 'And there's nothing like belief in the lie you tell yourself, is there?'

William Lundy didn't know what to say and found himself a little tongue-tied.

'No, no, I guess not,' he stammered, then asked, 'But how did you reunite with your son?'

'He tracked me down and turned up on my doorstep in '61. He was seventeen years old, and he returned to

Orleans and asked around. I was a prominent businessman and known about town and not hard to find, but when I opened the door I did get a surprise. I immediately knew it was him. He looked just like me when I was his age.'

'And then?'

'Then, luckily the war came along and we joined up and went in separate directions.'

'Why do you say *luckily*?'

'Because by then we were fighting like cats and dogs.'

'Was the disagreement over you leaving his mother?'

'No, it was just him and me, and that was the trouble. Speaking to Walter was like having a conversation with myself, only when I was seventeen. I'm twenty-seven years older than Walt, so by then I had already dismissed most of the hare-brained ideas he was putting forward. It was a relief when I joined in '62 and left him behind to look after the property. But he also joined up the following year and . . . ' A hand on Jason Taylor's shoulder stopped him mid-sentence. It was Ned.

'One of the women on the south-end watch said she saw something outside. The marshal sent me to get you.'

'Me?' said Taylor, a little surprised. Quietly he followed Ned out of the room and quickly down to the southern end of the long building.

In the gloom they found Walt with a young woman by his side, peering through a window. She was pretty with a warm but nervous smile and not much more than sixteen years of age.

'What is it?' asked Jason Taylor, crouching just behind the two of them.

'Emma was sure that she saw something over on the other side of the clearing. Emma, you want to tell Mr Taylor what you saw?'

'It looked like shadows moving about. Bent over.'

'How many?' asked Taylor.

'Three.'

'In what direction?'

The young woman paused and seemed a little confused.

'Right to left, left to right, forwards or backwards?' asked Walt.

'Right to left,' she said clearly.

'That would make sense,' said Taylor. 'Coming out of the thick brush and across to the south-west corner of the fort.'

'Emma, I want you to tell me and Mr Taylor what you can see in that dark brush to the right, now,' prompted Walt.

Emma spoke slowly but clearly. 'I can see the brush, its shape, the individual branches and the grass below it. And two small dark stones.'

Walt looked over at Jason Taylor.

'Was I right?' asked Emma. 'Is that what you can both see?'

Jason Taylor gently patted her shoulder and said, 'No, that's not what I can see. But at your age, when my sight was better, I could.'

'If you saw moving shadows then we

have company,' said Walt. 'It is probably a scouting party and you have now given us the opportunity to prepare, so thank you, Em.'

25

Skirmish at Dawn

Tuesday 30 August

The skirmish started on the south side of the building with the breaking of glass just at the first twilight of dawn. It was followed almost immediately by a shotgun blast that echoed through the empty building as if a giant hammer had struck the side of an empty water tank. The settlers, who were looking out of the window on the western side with Walt, jumped as one with fright, and the woman closest to him let out a gasp and clutched at his arm.

'Stay. Don't leave this window, and fire only when you have a target,' shouted Walt, just as he heard the shooting outside begin. With his rifle in his right hand he ran down through the length of the long building towards the firing. He could hear the thump of the lead rounds upon the timber walls. Wood fragmented into splinters as the bullets punched through the planks and filled the air of the drab interior with dust.

Now running fast and bent forward, he was almost to the door of the furthest room when, to his right, he caught a glimpse of a face looking through the window at him. Instinctively, he turned, half-raised his rifle to his shoulder and fired. The round struck the glass and the face was gone.

When he got to the door of the end room and pushed it fully open he was greeted by the gaze of four wide-eyed settlers, all crouched and hiding behind the corner of the stone fireplace. Glass broke and fell to the floor as a bullet zinged through the window and over Walt's head, to thump into the wall on the other side of the room.

'Stay down, stay down,' called Walt. He ran crouching to the corner of the smashed window. He jerked his head up, just in time to glimpse three figures disappearing into the dark of the brush.

The shooting stopped as abruptly as it had started, leaving just the frightened faces of the settlers.

'Were they trying to enter?' called Walt.

A woman spoke quickly in a high-pitched voice.

'I saw him, I saw him, his face, right before me, through the window, then he struck the glass to get in.'

In the early-morning light Walt could see specks of blood upon her cheeks and chin where she had been cut by the breaking glass.

'Who fired?' he called.

'I did,' called back one of the settlers. 'Don't know if I hit him or not.'

'That doesn't matter,' said Walt, still crouching. 'You surprised them and alerted us all. And that was your job. You have done well, all of you.'

'Is that it? Is it all over now?' asked the woman. 'Can we go? Can we leave?'

'No,' said Walt. 'That was just a scrap

with a scouting party, who now know that we are here, ready for them, and armed. They will return, but next time it will be in force.'

The look on her face was a mix of absolute bewilderment and stark terror. So Walt patted her arm and said, 'We will be fine, just fine. You have my word.'

Walt got up on his feet; the other three settlers all fixed their gaze upon him with the intensity of brethren at a church service seeking a pastor's blessing. He hesitated, then quickly averted his eyes in case they could see that he had just told a lie.

26

Innocent

First Light
Walt walked cautiously back along the length of the vacant building, checking from window to window to see that the ground out to the brush was clear. As he walked he spoke to settlers, huddled and on watch, encouraging them to remain alert and ready. He patted a shoulder and smiled in the hope that he would receive a smile in return, but he didn't. The display of fear on their silent faces was clearly visible.

It was not until he was near the northern end of the building that he heard the sound of murmuring coming from one of the rooms. He eased open the door to see an older woman on her knees, cradling the covered head of a limp body that lay upon the floor.

As he approached the woman looked up and he could see the tears streaming down her cheeks as she quietly wept. He knelt down near where blood had puddled by the side of the body, reached over and gently grasped the limp but still-warm hand. He lifted the arm to expose a bloody wound where the bullet had entered the side.

'How?' Walt said, but the weeping woman did not answer. He looked around to find where the bullet had come from, and could see a spot of early daylight that was now visible through the hole in the wall. A shot from outside the building had punched through the wall, down low and close to the floor.

He looked up at the distraught woman to offer comfort, but could think of nothing to say. Then the folds of the woman's dress fell away from her bended knees to uncover the pale and frozen face of death. It was Emma.

Walt sucked back a quick breath as he felt his stomach roll into a bottomless pit. He quickly bit at his lips to stifle his curse.

'She was our clever one,' said the woman, her face crumpled in pain. 'She could read and write, and she was so innocent.'

Walt desperately wanted to say something of comfort, of consolation, but there was nothing that he could think of, only the overwhelming feeling of emptiness and a raging fire of anger.

27

Impulsive

An Hour Later

'The settlers want to throw themselves on the mercy of Cobos,' said Jason Taylor.

'They will get none,' said Walt, his voice sharp.

'I know, but they are scared and don't believe they can fight off another attack. They have lost what little courage they had from the engagement with the scouting party and the death of young Emma. And you can't blame them.'

Walt was silent.

'They have voted on it, and all agree. They even have a white flag they want to hoist, so that they may talk to Cobos and secure their release.'

'Secure their release? How? Do they

want to pay him for their lives?'

'They have no money, Walt. They are hoping that Cobos has a Christian heart.'

Walt cursed their naivety, then cooled down a little.

'Just say they were able to go, then that would leave me, Ned and Bill with Wheeler. Four of us in a last-ditch stand against what could be a hundred or more. It would just be one of us at each corner of this building. Geezes, we wouldn't even get to die in the company of each other.'

Taylor smiled at Walt's misplaced humour. 'At least you'd have me and Marie with you. So that makes six.'

Walt looked up, his eyes squinting a little as he stared at Taylor.

'You would stay?'

'Of course.'

Walt was touched by this unexpected sense of duty from his father.

'I could even hold your hand.'

Walt raised an eyebrow.

'Besides,' said Taylor, 'after Cobos

has killed us he's only going to ride after the settlers and kill them anyway.'

Walt shook his head. 'You never know when to quit, do you? For a moment there you were in front.'

Taylor nodded. 'True. It has been a lifelong failing of mine. But I am compensated with other more admirable characteristics.'

'Really, and what would they be?'

'Well . . . ' Jason Taylor now seemed lost for words. 'Well . . . ' he repeated.

'Well, what?' said Walt.

'Well, I can shoot straight.'

'Yeah, I'll grant you that,' said Walt.

'And so can Marie. So we should be useful to you.'

'We'll see about that,' said Walt. He picked up his rifle to leave. 'You know,' he said, 'the only reason I'm in this mess is because of you.'

Taylor thought for a little. 'I don't recall having invited you to come along. You chose to chase after me.'

'Yes, I did. More fool me.'

'That's because you're impulsive.'

'Yeah,' said Walt. 'I kind of get like that when my father has run out on me with my gold leases and my wife. I guess you could even call me reckless.'

'Oh, don't be so hard on yourself, Walter. Some of your weaknesses can be quite endearing. In fact, it reminds me of myself when I was your age.'

'So what are you saying? Now you tend not to be so rash any more, is that it?'

'Precisely,' said Taylor. 'Throughout our lives it is always best to stop, think and make a plan.'

'Plan? We could certainly do with one of those right now. So as soon as you have figured out what we need to do, just let me know.'

'Don't worry, son, I will.'

'And don't call me son,' said Walt, shaking his head in annoyance. 'I'd prefer not to be reminded that we are related.'

'Of course, Walter. Or should I call you Marshal?'

'Walt is just fine.'

28

A Front-Row Seat

Mid-morning

'You can raise your flag,' said Walt to Wesley Hefan.

'You're going to let them surrender?' asked Ned in disbelief.

'No.'

William Lundy was taking notes in his pad. He paused and asked, 'Are you going to let them talk to Cobos?'

'No, not that either.'

Both Ned and William stared at Walt with the same puzzled look.

'I'm not going to let anyone leave this building and speak to Cobos or any other bandit,' said Walt. 'It's too dangerous.'

'This is a truly confusing approach,' said Jason Taylor. 'Not to mention that it could be difficult trying to stop them, especially if Cobos rides up to our front door and wants to know what the white flag is all about.'

'That's what I'm counting on, Cobos riding up to our front door, but it won't be any of the settlers who will walk outside this building to talk to him. It will be me, and only me.'

'I should have guessed,' said Jason Taylor. 'A gallant gesture from a gentleman.'

Walt paid no attention to the comment. 'Wes,' he said, turning to a confused Wes Hefan, 'I know that the settlers don't want any part of this fight, but on this one you will have to trust me that I will look after everyone.'

'They all wish to leave,' said Wes firmly.

'And you?' asked Jason Taylor. 'They listen to you?'

Wes hung his head a little. 'They all know you are after Cobos. We have heard that you have papers for his arrest. But that has nothing to do with any of the settlers.'

'Yes,' confirmed Walt. 'I have papers to serve on Cobos. It came with the job when I signed on to be a US deputy marshal, but I am also well aware of my obligations to you and your settlers. What I have to do now is try and balance the two.'

'Is that possible?' William asked.

'Anything — ' But before Walt could finish, Jason Taylor interrupted with, 'Is possible.' He smiled, then continued, 'So you do have a plan, after all?'

Walt didn't answer the question. 'Just trust me on this one, Wes. Let me speak to Cobos.'

'And you will ask if he will let us go?'

'I will do all in my power to keep you safe.'

Wes seemed unsure but nodded his head slowly.

'And I need you to tell the settlers that they must not interfere in any way.'

Wes nodded, then said, 'I'll talk to them.' However, he spoke without any enthusiasm.

'No interference,' insisted Walt. 'You

can go ahead and raise your flag on the main flagpole, and Mr Taylor will provide security to those who are to go into the courtyard. Be quick, then return to your posts and continue to keep watch for Cobos.'

Jason Taylor went to speak, but paused. He left the room with Wesley Hefan.

As soon as the door closed Walt walked over to Ned and William.

'I am going to need the help of both of you for a scheme I have in mind.'

'So Jason Taylor was right, you do have a plan,' said William.

Walt ignored William Lundy's statement. 'Bill, I need you to find my saddle valise and take from it some papers marked with a C and bring them to me.'

'Now?' asked William.

'Now,' confirmed Walt. He waited until William had left the room.

'Ned, I need you to use your Sharps for me.'

'Ready any time,' said Ned.

'How accurate are you?'

'How accurate do you want me to be?'

'I want you to hit a target from about one hundred twenty, maybe one fifty paces away with one shot and on my signal. No second chance.'

'One twenty: that's short range for a Sharps. The sight only goes down to one hundred yards but up to one thousand. What size is the target?'

'Size of a melon.'

'A melon?'

'A melon with a hat on it. A Mexican hat.'

'You want me to shoot a Mexican in the head from about one hundred yards?'

'Yep.'

'What will this Mexican be doing?'

'Talking to me.'

'So he won't be a moving target?'

'No, but he will be sitting on his horse, so if his horse moves, then he moves.'

'Will I be lying down, sitting or

standing when I take this shot?'

'Don't know. Probably standing on a ladder with your arms supported. I want you to take your shot from the small belltower on the barracks roof. But first, I want you to climb into position and tell me where I need to stand on the ground at the front of this building, so that you can see me, unobscured by the roofline, and where you will have a clear line to any Mexican that I might be talking to.'

Ned scratched his chin. 'You want me to shoot a man in front of this building?'

'Right.'

'And you want me to do it with a headshot from a raised position about one hundred yards away?'

'Yep.'

'While he is sitting on his horse and you are talking to him?'

'Yes, but on my signal.'

'What will the signal be?'

'The serving of arrest papers.'

'On Cobos?'

'Right.'

'What if Cobos won't accept these arrest papers?'

'He doesn't have to accept them. I just have to deliver them. And I'm hoping that he won't know what they are until he gets them in his hand. And that, Ned, will be your signal to fire.'

'So, let me get this straight, I'm going to kill a man who you have papers to arrest.'

'That's right,' said Walt. 'But these arrest papers have marked him to be killed.'

'Is that within the law?'

'It's on my judgement and comes with a reward of one thousand dollars, and all of it is yours.'

Ned rubbed his whiskered chin. 'Lot of money. Do you think that I'll ever get to spend it?'

'To be honest, probably not.'

'And what are you going to do once I fire and shoot Cobos dead? He's bound to have company with him.'

'I'll have my handgun holstered with six rounds.'

'On a good day that would mean that you and me could account for seven, maybe eight as I can probably reload and fire before you get all your shots away. But Wheeler said there could be one hundred in all with Cobos, so what do we do about the other ninety-two?'

Walt shrugged. 'Not sure, but do young renegade Indians really want to kill settlers?'

'Don't know.' Ned pulled on his whiskers in thought. 'The distance and elevation is not difficult. Nor is the size of the target. Not from that range, it's close, real close for a Sharps, so I'd be better off taking the shot with a repeating rifle, that way I can get a few more shots in after you have fired your six shots.'

'No, my plan calls for the use of firepower. I want that big .52-calibre bullet to hit its mark. I want your shot to cause the maximum surprise in those who observe it. I want them to see and feel the terror of an unexpected violent death, up close. I want it to panic those who ride with Cobos into thinking that they could be next.'

'It will do that all right,' said Ned, looking closely at Walt. 'And just where did you get the idea for this plan of yours?'

'From your buffalo story.' Walt hesitated, then asked, 'Have you ever done anything like this before, Ned?'

Ned continued to pull slowly on his whiskers.

'Yes, during the war, but not at a range this close. Back then we would crawl close to the perimeter of the federals' rest camps and take them by surprise. But when you shoot a man in the head with a Sharps .52, even from way out, you still get to see what happens.'

He gently stroked his beard. 'The head explodes, but it's not just death. I've seen what it does to the men who are next to the man I marked. Sometimes, I would select a target within a group where they were all tight and close, just resting and conversing amongst friends. Then, when I squeezed that trigger it would all change in an instant. They are suddenly soaked in a shower of blood and covered with small particles of brain and bone.

'Their peace is shattered. Most just freeze in shock, initially. One second a life, a friend, next a twitching corpse with half a head. Fright finally kicks in and they scramble for cover on all fours, fearing that they will be next.'

'I've heard those same stories, but I've never seen it,' said Walt.

'If this scheme of yours works, you're going to see it all right. You're going to see the most gruesome of spectacles and you're going to see it from a front-row seat.'

29

A Little Hazy

Midday

'Just there,' said Ned, 'that flat stone near the wheel rut. I can see that from the belltower with my arms resting on the sill. If you are standing anywhere beyond that point, then I will be able to see all of you. If you stand back closer to the building, even by just a little, then it's going to be difficult. I may see the back of your head and maybe your shoulders, but the stone is your mark if I am to see you from head to toe.' Ned's eyes smiled at Walt as if to say, *Have you got that? Is it clear?*

Walt looked out of the window, his eyes fixed on the small insignificant stone.

'You could see that from over on the roof of the barracks?'

'Yep.'

Walt was still looking at the tiny rock with amazement. 'It's only little.'

'Nothing wrong with my eyesight,' said Ned, as if it were in question.

'I can see that. So, I need to get off the veranda, past the picket fence, out in the open and up to that little stone?'

''Bout that, or a little before,' confirmed Ned. 'But that's your mark. I should get my first glimpse of your hat about ten paces back from that spot.'

'It's not a lot of room for Cobos and his band to squeeze into, is it?'

'It's enough,' said Ned. 'He won't want to get too close, at least at first, and it might help to crowd 'em up a little and make a sort of collective target.'

'Won't that make your shot harder?' asked Walt.

'Nope, and it might help you when you use your handgun. If I have a clear line to the target, then it doesn't matter if they are all standing shoulder to shoulder. When I work buffalo they crowd together and I'm at three, four, five or even six hundred yards out, sometimes more, depending on the terrain. The distance to the edge of the brush is just on one hundred.

'But,' said Ned, while his hand rubbed at his whiskers, 'the only thing that I need to know is, which one is Cobos?'

'The one I'll be talking to.'

'But I won't be able to hear him or you. You'll have your back to me and he may just be listening.'

Walt thought for a moment. 'You're right. We need to talk to Wheeler,' he said. 'Because I don't know what Cobos looks like, other than from a general description and that he's Mexican and has other Mexicans with him.'

Ned's blue eyes smiled. 'Maybe he'll be wearing the biggest sombrero?'

'An *hombre grande*, eh? But somehow I don't think so.'

'Then maybe he'll ride forward on his own? Show he's the man in charge. Even if he does it just by a yard or two, that would help.' Ned scratched at his whiskered chin again. 'But what if he doesn't want to talk to you right there, on that spot out there? If I'm stuck up that little tower on a ladder with just my head sticking out, and he moves too far left or right — or worse, up close, then I won't have any chance to get into a new position. I'm like a cork in a bottle up there.'

Walt ran his tongue across a dry bottom lip. 'I've asked Wes to paint a sign across the front of the building, saying that they are peaceful settlers and want to talk. So hopefully Cobos will present at the front door.'

'Will that work?'

Walt shook his head. 'Ned, I really don't know, but it's the only plan I've got.'

The door opened as William Lundy entered the room with Walt's valise over his arm and the warrant papers in his right hand.

'The valise was with your rifle scabbard in the cell. Wes Hefan had put it there to be safe.' He passed them to Walt, who could see that William had something on his mind.

'What is it?' Walt asked.

William hesitated. 'I . . . I saw the other papers for Frank Allen and Louis Bolan.'

'So?'

'I didn't mean to pry.'

'Join the crowd,' said Walt. 'Everybody here now seems to know all of my business, so why not you? The settlers are already having a field day with the gossip of me, my father and his new wife.'

Ned cackled. 'You can bet on that.'

'Did you see my expenses log in the valise there as well?' asked Walt.

'I did,' said William, a little embarrassed.

'Did you fill it in for me?'

'No,' said William emphatically.

'Pity, it's way behind and I'm going to have a devil of a time trying to make up enough stuff to suit. I could have done with some help.'

Ned let out another cackle at Walt's humour, but William Lundy was unsmiling.

'Do these papers mean that you can just shoot Cobos?'

'What makes you think that?' asked Walt.

'It says they can be served, dead or alive, on your judgement.'

'You *did* have a good look, didn't you?' Walt cast a glance in Ned's direction and went on, 'If Eloy Cobos was to ride up to our front door and voluntarily accept arrest, so that I could cuff him and ride him over to Fort Smith for trial, all peaceful-like, then the civil thing to do would be to take him in alive, wouldn't it?'

William thought for a moment before replying, 'But he's not going to do that. He's a murderer. He's slaughtered men. If he was taken back to Fort Smith he'd be hung, wouldn't he?'

'If the law is just, then you would expect so. Mind you, I've been told that justice on the Arkansas circuit is fickle and open to bribery, so he may get off. What do you think, Ned? Likely or unlikely that Cobos would come along if I asked him?'

Ned gave a wink in return, unseen by William, then thought for moment.

'Unlikely would be my guess.'

'So,' said William, 'in theory at least, you could shoot down Cobos in cold blood and just say that you served him the arrest papers and that he refused to accept them?'

Walt jerked his head back a little in mock indignation.

'Now that's a novel idea, Bill.'

Ned chuckled. 'Now that would be shenanigans, wouldn't it?'

'No,' said William, 'I'm just saying . . . '

'Saying what, precisely?' asked Walt. 'That people like Cobos don't deserve to live?'

William took in a breath and lifted his shoulders.

'Not amongst peaceful citizens, no he

doesn't. Not if he wants to do them harm.'

'What do you think, Ned?'

'Young Bill's view could have merit, now I come to think about it.'

Walt raised his eyes as if in contemplation.

'Yeah, me too,' he said. 'I would think that's a pretty fair appraisal, but I still plan to speak to him anyway and see what he has to say.'

'So are you going to serve these papers on him?' asked William.

'Yep, that's the idea. But I don't want anyone else to know that's the plan.'

'But he won't accept them, will he?' said William.

'No, I'm guessing not.'

'So, what then?'

'I then have the authority vested in the warrant to kill him.'

'But if you do that, you will be shot down in revenge by those who ride with him.'

'Maybe, but Ned and I have a plan of sorts to seize the moment by surprise and use it to our advantage. And I want you to be part of it.'

'Is it dangerous?' William's voice was a little shaky and failed to disguise his concerns.

'Bill, if Cobos turns up, and I believe he will, then the situation for every one of us will be dangerous. What happened at first light this morning was no more than a brief scrap; and being in this old fort with so few experienced shooters offers little protection, especially if it is set on fire to smoke us out.'

The colour in William's face seemed to drain as he repeated the word, 'Fire.' The realization of what might lie ahead was now etched in his fearful expression. Bill stiffened his back and looked at Walt.

'What do you want me to do?'

'I want you to go with Ned and provide him with protection, should he need it.'

'You can also act as my spotter,' said Ned. 'A shooter always needs a spotter.'

'And what do I have to spot for you

to shoot?' asked William, looking at Ned.

Ned looked to Walt to answer.

'Cobos,' said Walt. 'The plan is to shoot Eloy Cobos dead in front of his men with one shot from Ned's big-bore Sharps rifle.'

William seemed a little flustered, his mouth opening and closing before he said, 'I understand, but then what? How do we deal with his gang of savages?'

'That,' said Walt, rubbing his chin, 'I have to admit is where the plan is a little hazy, so I'm still working on it.'

30

Gone

Late Afternoon

'Wheeler has gone.'

Walt looked up while chewing on a thin strip of salted beef. 'Gone where? I need to talk to him about Cobos.'

Wes shrugged. 'Don't know where. He's just left, and he's taken one of your horses as well.'

Walt stopped chewing. 'When?'

'We guess about an hour, not much more,' said Wes. 'Adam's young boy saw him leave, but he's only just told his mother.'

'Are you sure? Has anyone checked?'

'I have,' said Adam Reed, standing in the doorway with his young boy beside him, who was not much more than four or five. 'I've been looking. His horse, saddle and belongings have all gone,

240

along with one of your mounts but not one of your saddles.'

'Did he take the one with the government brand?' asked Walt.

'Don't know,' said Reed. 'I didn't see.'

'Could be for the best,' said Jason Taylor. 'If Cobos wants Wheeler and he's not here, he'll have to go and find him, and leave us alone.'

Walt stayed silent, still holding the stick of dried beef upright in his hand.

'You don't agree?' said Taylor, trying to get a response.

Walt finally said, 'Don't know.'

'Maybe it was an honourable act,' said Wesley Hefan. 'Maybe he did it to keep the women and children safe?'

'Maybe,' said Walt but his tone suggested he thought otherwise.

Taylor fixed his stare on his son.

'What is it?'

Walt didn't answer.

'Are we off the hook now, with Wheeler gone?' asked Wes.

'Guess that depends,' said Walt slowly. 'If Cobos is just after Wheeler . . . If it is just a personal vendetta against one man.'

'But you're not convinced, are you?' said Taylor.

'Not if he's trying to cover up the killing of Louis Bolan and his men, or . . . ' Walt stopped.

'Or what?' asked Taylor.

Walt looked up at Jason Taylor. 'Or wanting to set up another massacre that will let the cavalry loose against the surrounding Indian nations.'

All eyes were upon Walt, who sat hunched forward on an upended small wooden box.

No one spoke until Taylor said, 'You don't see any good in Cobos, do you, Walter? And you, a man who loves Mexico and all things Mexican.' He paused, then continued to mock: 'Maybe it was just the tequila you liked after all?'

Walt looked at his father. 'Just put a cork in it.'

'Will Cobos come, Marshal?' asked Wes.

'I expect so, but I guess we'll just have to wait and see.'

'For how long?' asked Wes.

'I guess a day, maybe two, but no more.'

'Maybe we should go while we can?' suggested Adam Reed.

Walt slid the half-chewed stick of beef into the top pocket of his shirt.

'I'd say the chances of getting past any Indian scouts are next to none. I'd also expect that they have been keeping an eye on us since we interrupted their scouting party, and would have seen Wheeler leave. What do you think, Ned?'

'Think the same,' said Ned.

'If we are being watched, then why did he leave, and in broad daylight?' asked William.

'I'd say he got spooked and panicked,' said Ned. 'Seen men do senseless things when they take fright.'

'He's been keeping to himself and

brooding of late,' said Wes.

'Well, none of us have been exactly welcoming of his presence since he came clean, have we?' said Walt.

'Will he try and make it back to Henrietta?' asked William.

'My boy saw him leave to the north, not south,' said Adam Reed.

'Wherever he's running to he'll be running fast to get out of the Territory, but hoping like hell that he'll make it to nightfall first, I'd say,' said Ned.

'Will he make it?' asked William.

'Only if he's very lucky,' said Walt.

'It may just draw Cobos away from us,' offered Taylor.

'I'll give it one more night, but no more. Then I'm going,' said Adam Reed with defiance, and he left the room.

Walt was silent again and deep in thought.

'Marshal? Mr Reed said he would give it just one more night,' said William.

'I heard,' said Walt.

'Can you do something to stop him

from making a rash decision?'

'Like what, Bill? What do you want me to do, cuff him to a hitching rail? I'm a deputy marshal, not a nursemaid. We must each make our own decisions. Who knows, Pat Wheeler may get to Kansas safe and sound. Only time will tell.' Then he added, 'But I wouldn't bet my life on it.'

31

Missing

Wednesday 31 August — Before First Light

A hand shook Walt awake. He'd been dreaming of the time when he first met Maria, and of the silhouette of her figure against the glow of the cantina lamps as she danced. He could hear the heels of her shoes stomping upon the hard wooden floor and the crisp click of the castanets.

She had just turned to him and whispered, 'Walter, Walter my love,' and he was just about to say, 'Yes, my darling?' when Wesley Hefan's hand shook him again. Walt looked up at Wes leaning over him. 'Geezes,' he said under his breath.

'Now Adam Reed is gone,' said Wes with urgency.

'He has left already?' asked Walt, trying to clear his head.

'No, he's gone missing. His family were ready to leave, but they are still here. He went out to hitch his wagon and he hasn't come back. His wife is concerned.'

Walt propped himself up on one arm and reached out for his canteen.

'Was anybody with him?'

'No.'

Walt twisted on the cork stopper. 'Has anyone looked?'

'His wife went to look but I stopped her,' replied Wes.

'Good.' Walt took a mouthful of water, swallowed, then ran the dirty cuff of his shirtsleeve across his mouth. 'I'll go take a look.'

'I'll come with you,' said Taylor from the doorway.

'You here too?' mumbled Walt. He took another mouthful of tepid water. 'No, best just one of us goes. Did anybody hear anything? Any noise?'

'Nothing.'

Walt sat up and slowly pulled on a boot.

'You look done,' said Taylor.

'It's all this clean living,' said Walt. 'It's killing me. I need a drink.'

'Know how you feel,' said Taylor.

'You do? What happened to that new leaf?'

'Ah, yes, the new leaf. You can turn over more than one, you know.' Taylor sounded jovial and it was grating on Walt.

'How practical!'

'That's me.'

'Hand me my other boot.'

His father reached over and tossed the boot at his son. Walt caught it.

'What are you doing up so early, anyway? It's not your shift,' he asked.

'A fit and healthy man needs little sleep,' Taylor said.

'How pleasing. Why don't you go and look for Reed and leave the unfit and unhealthy to sleep?'

'OK,' said Taylor. He turned to go, then said, 'What if I don't come back?'

Walt was undecided as to whether he should put the second boot on or take the first one off.

'What?' he said.

'I said, what if I go out there and don't come back?'

Walt seemed totally uninterested in his father's question as he stared at his foot with the big toe protruding through a hole in the sock.

Taylor was undeterred and continued as if giving a performance to a theatre audience.

'Scooped up in the black of night by Indian spirits seeking revenge against the white man for dispossessing their kin of their land, to then be wisped away to a place beyond the reach of mortals. So what say ye as I prepare to leave on a task from which I may not return?'

With a grunt, Walt pulled on his second boot and mumbled, 'May we all live in hope of such a blessed event.'

★ ★ ★

Walt might have had his boots on, but he was not up and standing in them. He had rolled back on to his blanket, lain his head upon his valise and closed his eyes for just a moment. *A few seconds*, he told himself, *and then I'll get up*; but he didn't, instead he fell asleep.

However, Maria in her flamboyant dress with the swishing folds of black and red fabric failed to reappear. This time it wasn't a hand that shook him awake, but the sound of a soft low whistle. Its familiarity jerked him into a sitting position; he'd heard it often. It was a signal of warning from his father. He sat, straight-backed, and wondered how long he'd been asleep. Then he quickly groped about to touch the smooth leather of his gunbelt. He lifted it gently with one hand and stood up.

The quiet whistle came again from just outside the building, just below the window of the room where Walt stood. He cautiously stepped towards the wall and crouched. Then he lightly tapped a knuckle twice against the rough timber wall.

A tap-tap was returned almost immediately, and he got the message. He carefully made his way to the door of the room, then turned left down the dark corridor. When he was almost at the door that led to the cookhouse and the courtyard he saw a shadow before him. It was Wes Hefan.

Walt leant in close so that Wes could see the outline of his face as he put a finger to his lips. Wes nodded, then slowly followed on behind Walt for the last few steps to the door.

Walt slowly lifted the wooden latch, then eased the door open gently. He turned to Wes and motioned for him to stay and close the door behind him, pointing to the latch so that he would know to lock the door. Wes nodded back.

Walt stepped into the night air. He then crept down along the side of the building to where his father had sent his signal and almost fell across the crouched figure of Jason Taylor before he saw him.

'Easy,' said Taylor softly.

Walt went down on one knee and whispered, 'What is it?'

Taylor held up his hand to silence Walt, then pointed out into the courtyard.

Walt looked but couldn't see or hear anything. He quietly asked, 'Have you seen any sign of Reed?'

'No, but we've got company.'

'Another scouting party?'

'More this time.'

'How many more?' asked Walt.

'I've stopped counting,' whispered Taylor.

'Well, now that I'm here, let's take one more look for Reed.'

Walt tapped his father's shoulder and was about to edge past him when a group of six to eight figures ran across the courtyard. Walt froze and watched as their fast feet barely made a sound upon the quadrangle before the shadows were swallowed up into the night.

'Where did they come from?' he said under his breath.

'Better we go back,' said Taylor, 'and quick.'

Walt turned and counted the steps back to the door where he tapped and called quietly, 'Wes, let us in.'

The door opened. Walt waved his father through, then quickly followed.

'What did you see?' asked Wes, his voiced pitched slightly high.

'Indians,' said Taylor as he sat down upon the floor. 'Lots of Indians.'

Wes's eyes seemed to bulge.

'Get everyone up, in position, and on alert,' said Walt.

Wes turned quickly, scraping a boot across the floor.

'And quietly,' called Walt softly after him. He rolled back to sit with his back against the wall. 'What do you think they are doing out there? Just looking?'

'Don't know,' said Taylor, 'but they could have had us by now. Maybe they are just figuring out what buildings are occupied and what buildings are empty.'

'For an attack, at dawn?' asked Walt.

'If they were federals I'd say so, but I don't know how Indians fight. Do you?'

Walt shook his head. 'Did you see any sign of Adam Reed out there? Anything?'

'No, and I had a good look around his wagon and the stables before I saw our first group of visitors.' Taylor pushed his back up against the wall to sit next to Walt. 'So what do you think?'

'I just hope they're not collecting firewood to burn us out,' said Walt.

'Is that what you'd do if you were them?'

'Seems like an easy way.'

'Well, fortunately I didn't see any sign of firewood-collecting.'

'We'll know soon enough. It's starting to get light.'

'A new day,' said Jason Taylor.

Walt said nothing.

'You are supposed to say back, maybe the last day, remember?'

'Yeah, I remember, but it seemed a little too close to the bone.'

'Now don't you go getting all serious, Walter. You know that nothing is ever as good or as bad as it seems.'

'I'll try to remember,' replied Walt. 'You stay here and mind the door. I've got to go and get Ned and Bill.'

'What for?' asked Jason Taylor.

'It's just something we worked out and I need them to be in position while we still have time.'

'Anything I need to know about?'

'No, not really, you'll only worry.'

'Not me,' said Taylor. 'I do my best not to worry about anything, or haven't you noticed?'

'Yeah, I've noticed,' said Walt, 'and it annoys the hell out of me.'

32

Surrounded

Just Before First Light

William had left in a hurry, close behind Ned, after hearing the instructions from Walt to take up their position in the small belltower. In his haste he grabbed his notepad and stuffed it down the front of his shirt, then slid two pencils into the pocket of his trousers. Then he followed Ned out through the door.

It was only when he was standing at the bottom of the first ladder into the ceiling of the barracks, and was handing up Ned's long and heavy Sharps rifle, that he remembered his pistol. The Colt Navy that had been given to him by Walt and was to be used to protect Ned, was back beside his bedroll where he had placed it after doing his night watch.

'I've got to go back,' said William to Ned. 'I've left the pistol behind.'

'Can't now,' said Ned. 'No time and it's getting light. You'll be seen crossing from the barracks to the cookhouse.'

'But I didn't see anyone in the courtyard,' protested William Lundy. 'And it will only take a moment to retrieve.'

'No,' said Ned, his voice whispered but stern. 'You can use my pistol. I need you up here.'

Ned's tone made it clear where William's duties lay, so the journalist just said, 'Yes, Ned,' a little like a scolded schoolboy.

The ladder from the barracks floor was not directly below the belltower. It reached to the ceiling and into the roof cavity; from there a narrow, one-plank-wide boardwalk stretched for some twenty paces to a second ladder directly below the belltower. This ladder was narrower than the first and almost vertical, with its legs straddling a small opening where the ropes from the bell had once hung down into the barracks.

Ned eased himself up on his bandy legs and once again called for his rifle. As William went to hand it up he almost dropped it. Ned looked down and cursed.

'Treat my Sharps with respect,' he called quietly but harshly. 'It once belonged to a Union boy who gave his life owning it.'

William gripped the weapon tight with reverence and stepped up another rung on the ladder. As he passed it up to Ned, who was now in the confined space of the belltower, he could smell the linseed oil upon the smooth dark butt of the weapon, and wondered how many men this rifle had killed.

'Now you come up, nice and easy,' called Ned softly.

When William eventually got to squeeze past Ned and push his head above the edge of the belltower it had been with considerable difficulty, as the space was tight and the ladder really only provided purchase for one man.

'Your knee's on my hand,' said Ned, pulling it free.

'Sorry, Ned,' said William. 'It's just that there's not much room for the two of us, and a pencil is sticking into my leg.'

Ned shook his head, unseen by William. 'Ease yourself back, Bill, sit on the ledge behind you and brace your foot on the ladder below my arm.'

William squeezed against Ned, then lifted himself on to the narrow ledge.

'How's that?' asked Ned.

'OK, I guess,' came the hesitant reply.

'Can you see out OK without lifting your head too high?'

William looked around. 'Not a lot. Ned, this is not very comfortable.'

'Never is,' said Ned. 'But I've been in worse. Lots worse.'

'What do I do now?'

'I can see out to my front,' said Ned. 'You need to look out behind me and to the sides.'

'What for?'

'Anything. Just tell me.'

'Tell you anything I see?'

'That's right. Anything you see.'

'What good is that?'

'Bill, don't test me. We have a task to do. You tell me and I'll understand, OK?'

'OK, Ned.'

'Then start, I can look and hear at the same time. I'm not that decrepit, yet.'

'No, of course not, Ned,' said William with respect. 'It . . . it's still quite dark, and . . . and I can't see a lot.' He stopped his short commentary and there was silence.

Ned let out a soft snort. 'This is not some foolish notion of mine. I need to keep my eyes on the ground ahead at all times. I want you to see where I can't look. So, relax and start with the horizon and work in to the closest ground.'

William drew in a breath. 'I can just see the skyline and the dark shapes of the brush, but not much else.'

'You will soon, it'll get light real quick. Move your eyes from left to right, then back to where you were first looking.'

William tried it. 'Oh, yes, I can see some rocks now. Some tall rocks.'

'Yeah, I can see those rocks too,' said Ned.

'Ned?'

'What?'

'I was sure that I just saw one of those rocks move.'

Ned hunched forward, looked down over the top of the barrel of his rifle and examined the ground in front of him.

'Yep, they can do that.'

'How?'

'Because those rocks are Indians.'

William's foot slipped on the rung of the ladder.

'Easy,' whispered Ned. 'No noise and only slow, deliberate movements.'

'Can you see them too? Where?'

Ned's voice was calm. 'To my front.'

'But they are on this side as well. Lots.'

'Keep looking around,' said Ned.

William slowly turned his head, then gripped at his small ledge seat and nearly fell off his perch.

'Ned,' he said in an excited whisper. 'I can see more.'

'Easy, easy, I can see them too.'

'They look just like a picket fence that has surrounded the fort.'

'It's the renegades,' said Ned calmly. 'So Cobos is here somewhere, but where?'

33

Which One is Cobos?

First Light

As the faint light of the new day slowly turned the dark night sky from a shade of ink blue to pastel pink, before the first glorious crimson glow of dawn, Walter Garfield and Jason Taylor crouched and watched. But it was not the magnificence of an Indian Territory sunrise that captured their attention from the small window of their fragile fortress. Instead, it was a ring of Indian warriors, each silhouetted in the rising light and each armed with a rifle cradled in his arms.

'Geezes,' said Walt quietly.

'Don't see that every day, do you?' said Jason Taylor. 'Guess they're out the back, too?'

'Guess so,' said Walt softly.

'Would seem that they are expecting us to surrender; all standing there in the open and just waiting for us to come out.'

The floorboards creaked as Wesley Hefan crept over and knelt behind Walt.

'We can see Indians out on the other side,' he said, a little out of breath.

'Out front too,' said Taylor.

'So, what do we do?'

'Just don't shoot,' said Walt, turning his head quickly to make eye contact with Wes. 'If someone shoots and our callers open fire on us, we're all dead. The sign out front and the white flag says we want to talk to them and that's what I plan to do.'

'Callers? Now that's a quaint name for them,' said Jason Taylor. 'Just like a home call from neighbours.'

'What if it is just the renegades?' said Wes.

'I doubt it,' said Walt. 'I don't think we have anything that the renegades want. They have been armed by Cobos and he is out there somewhere, so we just have to wait until he shows up.'

Wes lifted his head a little to look out of the corner of the window.

'More coming,' he said.

Taylor raised his head slowly to see, then put his hand on his son's shoulder.

'More neighbours. The welcoming committee has arrived.'

Walt looked out and saw five horsemen ride forward out of the edge of the brush, in a line, to stop in the open.

'You want to talk?' a Mexican voice shouted. 'Then come out and talk.'

'Which one is Cobos?' asked Walt.

Jason Taylor squinted a little. 'The one in the middle, I guess.'

Walt took in a short breath. 'OK, let me talk to him,' he said as he stood and felt inside his shirt for the warrant for the arrest of Eloy Cobos, but it wasn't there. 'The papers,' he said, a little flustered, 'I need the papers.'

'What papers?' asked Taylor.

Walt didn't answer but turned quickly and crossed to the room where he'd been sleeping. He grabbed at the valise frantically and released the buckle, but the papers were not inside.

'Geezes, not now, not now,' he said in protest as he leant down to toss back his bedding, searching. He knew that he'd had the warrant when in this room, but still there was no sign of the papers before he gave the crumpled blanket a final shake and the document with its ribbon fell to the floor.

'Thank you,' he said in prayer. As he turned in haste to leave the room he saw his old revolver lying next to where William had been sleeping. He picked it up and pushed it in behind his gunbelt, against the small of his back with the barrel tucked into the top of the trousers. He then grabbed his rifle and made for the door.

'They called again,' said Wes.

'Where have you been?' asked Taylor. 'The Mexicans are getting agitated.'

'I had to get something,' said Walt as he caught his breath. 'Open the door for me. No, stop. I need to check.' He quickly felt for the papers, which he had slid inside his shirt; then he reached down and touched the grip of his Smith & Wesson.

'Ready now?' asked Taylor.

'Yes,' said Walt. Then just as the door started to open he glanced down and saw his badge. With fumbling fingers he took it off and slid it into the top pocket of his shirt.

Jason Taylor held the door open as his son passed through. That was when he caught sight of the second pistol tucked in behind the small of Walt's back.

'Are you sure you are just going to talk?' he asked softly.

But Walt didn't answer as he stepped forward and into the early-morning light. He stopped to stand on the veranda and face the five horsemen, who were flanked by a line of renegade Indians.

'You stop there,' came the call.

'I want to talk,' called Walt.

'You can talk, but not armed. Your

flag says that you have surrendered. So put down your rifle and take off your gunbelt.'

Walt took a step forward. 'Then I'll be unarmed, while you will be armed,' he called.

'We have not surrendered,' came the call from the Mexican in the middle of the five. 'But you have.'

Walt slowly knelt as his mind raced; he laid his rifle down on the veranda. While still kneeling he undid his gunbelt and laid it down carefully.

'Now you can come forward.'

Walt stood and started to walk slowly as the door behind him reopened and Jason Taylor came on to the veranda.

'Stop,' called the Mexican.

Walt stopped and glanced back over his shoulder to see his father now standing in full view.

'Geezes,' he said under his breath. 'What are you doing?'

'Just providing a little back-up,' said his father quietly.

'Who are you?' came the call from the Mexican.

'I'm this man's father,' said Taylor. He raised his hands to show his palms. 'I'm not wearing a gunbelt and I only wish to help.'

Wes peered out of the window at the two figures. Walt, forward on the edge of the veranda, and Jason Taylor, just off to one side. Two men, just feet apart, and each with a pistol tucked inside the back waistband of his trousers.

Walt slowly stepped down off the veranda and along the narrow path towards the gate in the picket fence. With each step his eyes searched for the small stone that Ned had pointed out to him. The point that he had to get to, so that Ned could see him give the arrest papers to Cobos.

'That will do. Just stay where you are, where we can see you,' came the call.

'I need to talk. The man you are after, Pat Wheeler, has left,' called Walt.

The Mexicans laughed. 'We know. We have Wheeler.' There was more laughter but not from the one on the left and directly in front of Walt.

'Do you have anyone else from our party?' called Walt. 'A man named Adam Reed?'

There was more laughter. 'We have him too.'

Walt took a step forward. 'Is he OK?'

'He is resting with us.' The laughter continued.

Walt took another step. 'Can we see him?'

'Why?'

'His family and friends are worried. They want to see that he is all right.'

'He is all right, you have my word.'

'Then please can we see him for his wife's sake.'

The Mexican to the front of Walt nodded his head just slightly to the one in the centre, who was doing the talking, and who said in response, 'I will show you.' He turned his head and waved a hand to those behind him.

Six men appeared from the brush. One was Adam Reed standing upright but looking pale. Another was Pat Wheeler who was being held up on his feet, his legs buckling and one foot turned in on its side. His face was bloodied and his shirt ripped. Four men, two each with Reed and Wheeler, kept a tight grip upon their prisoners. These guards were not Indians but Americans.

'Now you see both.'

The escorts went to turn back with their prisoners when Wheeler called from swollen lips.

'They've come for the women.'

A sharp, hostile blow to the side of the face silenced Pat Wheeler as he crumpled to his knees.

'Are you Eloy Cobos?' called Walt. He stepped through the open gate, his eyes searching for the small stone.

'What do you want with Cobos?'

'I have something for him.' Walt's eyes darted over the five Mexicans while a voice in his head shouted, *Which one? Which one is Cobos?*

'What do you have for Cobos?'

'Some important papers.'

'What important papers?'

Walt went to take one more step.

'You stay where you are.'

'They are gold-lease papers, worth a lot of money. Mexican El Oro gold-lease papers.'

'Where did you get these papers?'

'They are mine. Let me show you.' Walt took another step.

'You stop moving about.'

Walt caught sight of the little flat stone and felt his stomach roll. It was a dozen paces away, yet that small gap put paid to his plan, which now seemed futile and foolish. He knew that Ned would have the Mexicans in view, but who was the target, the Mexican in the middle or, as Walt suspected, the one before him who had nodded for the prisoners to come forward?

Walt's feet felt heavy as if glued to the ground. He was stuck at this spot and short of his mark. Ned would not be able to see him or his signal, and without that signal he could not identify Cobos.

'Let me show you the papers,' said Walt. He took two more steps forward, slowly slid his hand into his shirt and extracted the bundle with its ribbon tied across the letter C.

'Here,' he said. He held the papers high with an outstretched left arm and waved them a little. 'Take a look. You will see.' With that he took another two steps and tossed the papers forward to land with a flat smack upon the dirt, just beyond the small flat stone.

No one moved.

'They will make you rich,' said Walt, trying desperately to hold his composure.

Slowly the rider to the far right dismounted. He casually walked across to the papers and picked them up. He then turned towards the other four mounted horsemen and held out the papers, but not to the middle rider.

As Walt watched he could feel a trickle of sweat run down the centre of his back as the older Mexican directly to his front sniffed hard through flared nostrils and looked down at the offering.

The silent voice inside Walt's head now screamed: *Take them, reach down and take the papers, Cobos.* But the rider didn't move; he just looked down upon the papers that were held out to him, until at last he said, 'These are not gold-lease papers. I've seen papers like this before. These are warrant papers. I killed a marshal who tried to serve papers like this on me.'

The other four Mexicans laughed.

'Why are you serving me with arrest papers?'

'Because I'm a US deputy marshal,' said Walt.

'You don't look like a marshal.'

Walt slowly and carefully reached into his top pocket, pulled out his badge and clipped it to his shirt.

'You have a badge, but you still don't look like a marshal,' the Mexican mocked. 'You have no gun. And all marshals should have a gun. If you have no gun, you die.'

'I'm a special marshal,' said Walt. 'I was sent to find and deliver those papers to Eloy Cobos and him alone. They are different from other arrest papers.'

'How, different?'

'Take a look.'

The Mexican hesitated.

'They can be delivered to Cobos . . . ' said Walt, then stopped short.

Cobos slowly reached down and took the papers, lifting them close to his face so that they could be examined. Walt drew in a breath and started again.

'They can be delivered to Cobos either alive or — '

But before that final word could leave Walt's lips, a booming shot like a clap of thunder split the crisp morning air.

34

Talk to Me

At the Same Time
If force is power, then surprise is its
equal. The big heavy lead bullet from
the Sharps rifle could drop a 1,500-
pound bison dead in its tracks from 800
yards away. For a shot over a much
lesser distance, and one at such a puny
target as the size and weight of the
human head, then this force was greatly
over-matched to the task.

Ned's sight had at first been upon the
centre rider of the five, but he knew he
was just guessing that this was Cobos.
So, while he held the butt of the Sharps
to his shoulder and his rifle cocked
ready to fire, he kept both eyes open as
he looked just above the barrel at all
five possibilities. He then waited for
Walt to appear as they had planned, but

like most plans this one went awry. He never got to see Walt.

Ned thought that maybe William could leave the small belltower and crawl along the barracks roof, where he could then catch sight of Walt, and from there relay a signal as to whom to shoot by holding up his fingers with the appropriate number from one on the left to five on the right. But when he half suggested the idea, while still keeping his eyes fixed upon his intended targets, he could tell from the response that young Bill had no stomach for such heroics.

Besides, Ned told himself, the young reporter would probably fall off the roof, alert the target, and break his leg! So Ned did what he always did in uncertain situations: he took some deep breaths to stay calm, and waited.

As the minutes ticked by, however, Ned's composure started to give way to hints of panic, until events were to unfold in his favour. While he could not hear what was being said, except for the sound of laughter from the Mexicans, he knew that Walt was out there, somewhere, but obscured from sight by the roofline of the building to his front.

He could see the flat stone where Walt should be, which provided the lowest point of his view from the belltower, and he trusted that if Walt could not get to that point, then there was good reason. He also knew that Walt would do his best to make the signal, somehow.

If all else failed, he told himself, the centre man of the five Mexicans would die.

'Talk to me, Bill,' said Ned softly. 'Tell me what you see.'

William Lundy's lips were dry and when he spoke his voice seemed to crack a little.

'I see Indians, standing in a line to either side of the five Mexican horsemen,' he started. 'I think the middle one is talking, but I'm not sure. I now see two men coming forward under escort. One is . . . ' his voice went a little higher, 'good God, it's Adam.'

'Keep going,' ordered Ned, pulling the rifle butt back tight into his shoulder.

'The other is bloodied, I don't know who it is.'

'It's Wheeler,' said Ned.

'Wheeler?' exclaimed William and choked a little.

'Keep talking,' said Ned. 'The wind, the light, anything, just keep speaking to me.'

William's head was swimming as he fought to regain composure.

'The wind is light, very light, coming, I guess, from the . . . south, I think. The light is clear and becoming very bright.'

Then William said, 'I saw something white, just poking above the edge, the edge of the roof.'

'Got it,' said Ned. He lowered his cheek to rest lightly upon the stock and moved his finger from the second to the first trigger ready to fire. 'It's the marshal holding the arrest papers high so we can see them.'

'I can see them again,' said William with excitement. 'The papers have been thrown out before the horsemen. Can you see, Ned?'

'I see,' said Ned. He checked his breathing, paused, caressed then gently squeezed on the trigger.

'One of the men is going to get them. Now he's picked them up and he is handing them to — '

The sound of the rifle shot took William Lundy by complete surprise. He leaped into the air with a jolt and nearly fell off his perch in the belltower and back down the ladder, into the ceiling of the barracks. Fortunately, he was able to grip at a passing rung and arrest his fall. The sound was so loud it was as if his ears had been boxed, while a cloud of blue smoke with a pungent, sulphurous smell of burnt black powder filled his nostrils.

Ned remained rock steady as he observed the fall of his shot. Then slowly he lifted his cheek from the rifle stock and expelled the breath that he'd been holding.

'Did you hit the target, Ned?' called William in a high-pitched voice as he clung on to the ladder. 'Did you?'

He didn't receive an answer from the old marksman.

35

Reaper

Morning Sunlight, Dust and Gunsmoke

The shot was straight and true, if properly a fraction too high for Ned's liking. It struck the target just above the left eye and emerged at the base of the neck, to strike a second target: one of the Americans who was standing back from Cobos and next to Adam Reed. It struck him in the hip, pivoting him sideways in a spin to collapse to the ground with a startled shriek and a heavy thud.

The impact of the big, fast, spinning bullet jerked Cobos's head back just a fraction before the rear of his skull exploded from the immense force that punched into the soft grey tissue of his brain. Several large bone fragments flew into the air, while one, still held by skin and hair, flapped over to the side to cover his left ear. A spray of warm blood, brain and smaller bone fragments instantly showered those to the sides and rear of Cobos, causing them to recoil with horror and instantly brace themselves with eyes clamped shut.

The booted feet of Eloy Cobos remained in the stirrups, and for just a second or two he continued to sit upright in the saddle. Then, slowly at first, he crumpled and slumped to one side, his body turning and inverting until he was completely upside down, to fall head first to the ground. One foot remained attached to the saddle as his upturned, mangled and lifeless body, with eyes and mouth open, became twisted and distorted as his horse turned in small circles trying desperately to break free from its fallen rider. On the third turn Cobos's foot slipped free from his boot and the horse bolted.

Walt had placed all his hope and faith

in Ned that, when he fired, the shot would strike the right target. Yet, when it happened he felt no joy or even a sense of relief, just complete and absolute shock. He had seen the savagery of men shot at close range when in battle. He had heard stories of the Union Sharpshooters during the war and seen the weapon fired, but he had never witnessed such killing power and certainly not at such close range. The suddenness and ferocity of the impact caught him with utter surprise and made him wince. He let out an involuntary expletive. The violent image overwhelmed him for a moment until he was released from this spell only by two wild shots from the Mexicans, which cracked low over his head.

Instinctively his arm swung to behind his back. His hand pulled his old Colt from the waistband of his trousers and in one swift smooth action he engaged the first target. The shot struck the standing Mexican a brutal and lethal blow high on the side of the neck, just below the jaw, causing him to twist sideways half a turn, bend at the knees, then drop to the ground.

Jason Taylor, who knew nothing of Walt's plan, which now erupted before him with the impact of Ned's shot, went down on one knee and pulled his pistol from his waistband. With his right arm thrust out straight and supported by the grip of his left hand, he pressed his cheek to his shoulder, sighted along the length of his arm and down over his pistol barrel, to squeeze off his first shot. Gunsmoke obscured his vision for a second; then, as the blue haze swirled and cleared in the morning light he saw the empty saddle where his target had once sat.

In battle even the most experienced will tell you that events are confused, loud, chaotic, and frightening. Vision often narrows to a tunnel, as if looking down a long pipe, while the heart races so fast that it would seem ready to leap from the chest. But of all the chaos it is the noise that most remember, for ever.

The deafening blast of the gunshots strikes upon the ears like a giant ferocious metal drum that screams of danger. 'Take cover!' it shrieks and only the very best of men can retain enough composure to locate and accurately engage a target amongst the dust and smoke, and the scrambling bodies that frantically seek survival.

It will be later, when the physical effects of absolute fatigue start to take hold, along with the constant desire to quench a raging thirst, that the mind will wonder how anyone managed to survive. Yet, during this clash of fire the body seems to know no barrier, and that was how it was for Jason Taylor, who leaped from the veranda and jumped the picket fence to join his son.

Just who shot which Mexican, as all of the bodies were to receive more than just one gunshot wound when finally examined, no one will ever know. But by the end of the twelve shots that were fired by Walter Garfield and his father, Jason Taylor, all the Mexicans were dead. Their bodies lay sprawled and twisted upon the ground, seeping life and blood into the dirt of Indian country.

The fusillade of shots initiated by Ned's opening round, and all that followed, occurred in a little more than twenty seconds. It scattered the Indians, the Americans, and their two prisoners as all sought cover in a desperate effort to get away from the mayhem.

Then, as if by order, the violence stopped and there was silence. A voice from on high called loud and clear: 'Do not return fire, or I'll shoot.' It was Ned in the belltower. He then turned to William Lundy and said, 'Make your way along the roof and tell them again, just in case they didn't hear. And don't fall off.'

William climbed out on to the shingled roof with trepidation.

'Take it easy and you'll be fine,' said Ned, as William, with a foot on either side of the roof peak, waddled forward like a bandy-legged duck until he was at the end of the barracks where he stopped, and raised himself straight and tall to yell:

'Cease fire, cease fire, or Ned will shoot any man who raises his gun.'

There was no need for this second warning. The renegades had witnessed the death of Cobos and the killing of the other Mexicans. This was not their fight so they turned and left quietly, to disappear back into the brush. Nor was it the fight of the remaining Americans, who gathered up their wounded man, quickly mounted their horses and made their getaway.

What William Lundy, the newspaper reporter from New York, saw as he looked down from his perch through the dust and smoke as it cleared, was just four men still standing. The two to the rear were Adam Reed, who was now assisting a bloodied Pat Wheeler to stand upright; and to the front was US Deputy Marshal Walter Douglas Garfield to the left, and his father Jason

Taylor to the right. Between these four men were the five lifeless bodies of the Mexicans.

'Is the marshal OK?' called Ned.

William turned his head to one side and nodded.

'What can you see?' called Ned, a little frustrated as it was beyond him to climb out of the small tower and on to the roof. 'So, tell me what you can see,' he called again.

William took in the scene before him. It was one that he had never expected to see in a lifetime, and one he would never forget. He called back, 'I can see all the Mexicans.'

'What are they doing?' yelled Ned. 'What's happened to them?'

William stood and stared. Then he turned his head and called back to Ned.

'All of them are dead.'

'Go on,' yelled Ned. 'Talk to me.'

'It is as if . . . ' William drew in a breath, 'it is as if they had been struck down by the Grim Reaper himself.'

'Who?' yelled Ned. 'Who?'

'A reaper,' called back William. He looked down at the marshal, then repeated again softly, 'Reaper.'

36

What Now?

Thursday 1 September 1870 — Early Morning

'What are you going to do, Walter? Are you going back to Mexico?'

'No, I've got nothing to go back to there.'

'Then what? You have to do something.'

'What do you want me to do? Tag along to California with you?'

Jason Taylor stiffened a little. 'No, I didn't mean that.'

'No, I didn't think you did,' said Walt.

'You're a young man, Walter. You should start a new life, doing something.'

'I am doing something, or haven't you noticed?'

'Yes, but I thought this marshalling business was just to chase after me.'

'It was, at first, but . . . '

'But?'

'I'm kind of growing into it.'

'I can see that,' Jason Taylor conceded. He patted the side of Walt's upper arm. 'You might even get good at it, one day.'

Walt looked at his father and shook his head. 'Yeah, one day, I might.'

'So where do you go from here?'

'I'll take Pat Wheeler back to Henrietta and ride Bill back to Fort Smith. Then I'll head down to Fort Worth. Ned says he'll come along for company.'

'Then what?'

Walt thought for a moment. 'Well, I might just ask for a nice easy job, somewhere quiet and peaceful that doesn't really need a marshal. Somewhere I can walk around and lift my hat to law-abiding citizens.'

'Do they have jobs like that?'

'Don't know,' said Walt. 'I've only

been with the marshals for a month. First, though, Ned and me have some reward money to pick up, and then we are thinking of taking the stage on down to New Orleans for a little relaxation and fun. Might even celebrate my birthday in the Quarter with a bottle of French champagne or two.'

'I could come,' said Jason Taylor with some eagerness.

'No, you're a married man now. This trip that Ned and me have in mind is for unwed men.' Walt pulled on the brim of his hat as the breeze lifted his collar. 'And now that I have been unwed by the law and the church, then I'm a well and truly unwed man — '

'OK, OK,' interrupted Taylor impatiently, 'I get the point.'

A small grin passed over Walt's lips, but his father didn't see.

'Well?' said Jason Taylor.

'Well?' repeated Walt.

'You want to say goodbye to Marie, I mean Maria, alone, before you go?'

'No, best you do that for me,' said

Walt. 'Just tell her . . . ' He pressed his lips tight, then relaxed and said, 'No, best not say anything. Although, you could tell her to be careful about putting on extra weight. She must be eating too much of her own good cooking. I've noticed that she's getting a fraction paunchy.'

Jason Taylor shifted his eyes quickly to Ned, who slowly raised his gaze to the heavens and began to hum quietly.

'You leaving now?' he said abruptly, to change the subject.

Walt nodded.

'You look after yourself, then, son.'

'I will.'

Jason Taylor extended his hand and Walt shook it quickly, making brief eye contact before he walked away to join the others and mount his horse.

'Good luck,' the father called to his son.

Walt gave a wave of the hand as he, Ned, William Lundy and Pat Wheeler turned away and departed.

'You're not very close to your father,

are you?' said William, riding alongside the marshal. 'I guess it was the gold thing, and of course Marie being — ' He cut his words short and bit at his tongue, thinking it best to leave that matter well alone.

However, Walt seemed not to notice, to be lost in his own thoughts before he said, 'No,' without looking at William. 'That wasn't it at all.'

'What was it, then?'

Walt shrugged. 'We're just too alike, him and me, that's all.'

'But are you?' asked William. 'Are you really?'

'Yep,' said Walt. He glanced back to catch a glimpse of his father still standing there and watching them depart. 'Just like two peas in a pod.'